FIRST Semester

A CAMPUS TALES STORY

Q.B. TYLER

Copyright © 2018 by Q.B. Tyler

All rights reserved.

ISBN: 9781674488288

No part of this publication may be reproduced, distributed, or transmitted in any form or by any means, including photocopying, recording, or other electronic or mechanical methods, without the prior written permission of the publisher, except in the case of brief quotations embodied in critical reviews and certain other noncommercial uses permitted by copyright law.

This is a work of fiction. Names, characters, businesses, places, events, and incidents are either the products of the author's imagination and used in a fictitious manner Any resemblance to actual persons, living or dead, or actual events is purely coincidental.

Cover Design: NET Hook & Line Designs
Editing: Kristen—Your Editing Lounge
Interior Formatting: Champagne Book Design

FIRST Semester

Prologue
Skyler

"*LA VITA VA AVANTI*"

Or in English: "Life goes on." It's what my mother always says. It's a sentiment that I grew up hearing any time things seemed bleak. Whenever I felt the world at my back my mother would give me a day to wallow in self-pity before force feeding me a week's worth of lasagna, followed by a kick in the ass, and the affirmation that life did, in fact, go on. It wasn't until I traveled across the globe to the motherland and managed to fall in love and get my heart broken in the span of three months did I really understand the sentiment.

I rub the tattoo written in faint script trailing down my arm.

La vita va Avanti

My heart flutters against my ribcage as I think about riding on the back of a Vespa through the streets of Venice engorging in far too much pizza and pistachio gelato. Spending the nights making love under the skylight in the apartment my parents had rented for me. Everything about it felt magical. But I guess that's what every young girl says about her whirlwind romance with the sweet-talking Italian.

"God Sky, you're such a cliché." My older sister snickered after I'd returned home four months later, ten pounds heavier with a heart I swore was broken inside my chest. I'd flipped her off and proceeded to spend the next two days in bed—Mom offered me a one day grace period because I guess I really looked pathetic. But, sure enough, on that second day, my mother slammed my curtains open, made me the breakfast of champions—frittata and more fresh rolls than was acceptable for your daily carbohydrate intake—and told me to take on the world because *"La Vita va Avanti, Bella." Life goes on.*

It wasn't until I found myself staring up into the neon sign of the tattoo parlor, sipping the iced coffee from the best, tiny bakery in Connecticut, that I realized just how I would show the world and *myself* that I had moved on.

Armed with the belief that I was a strong independent woman who didn't need a man, I'd marched into the small shop, slapped my ID on the counter, and took control of my destiny.

My initial idea, a tattoo that read "men ain't shit," didn't get rave reviews. The male tattoo artist seemed to take issue with that. And swore one day I would too.

I guess.

He'd urged me to get one that meant something and not an impulsive reaction in response to pain or heartbreak, because one day I wouldn't hurt anymore. One day I wouldn't give a fuck about *he who shall not be named.*

"Heartbreak sucks, kid, but you'll love again." He'd told me as he crossed his tattooed arms, lines of reds and blues inking his olive skin.

It wasn't the same, but I heard the sentiment lurking behind the words.

Life goes on.

Ten minutes later, *La Vita va Avanti* was on my arm forever. My mother had a fucking fit.

Skyler

I LOOK AROUND THE ONE-BEDROOM APARTMENT JUST OFF CAMPUS that my parents got for me—an *I'm sorry but this is for your own good*. I'd wanted to forego another year of school, tackle another European country, or maybe visit South America, or Africa, or Australia—hell, really any other continent except the one I was born on. I still crave adventure, and I still crave it beyond the borders of the US of A. At nineteen, I'm not ready for college, after spending eighteen years in what felt like shackles—known as the American school system—and they had finally set me free. I'm not ready for another four years of homework and tests and waking up before 8 AM for anything that isn't to catch the sunrise *or McDonald's* breakfast. I'm over school. That, coupled with the fact that I'm smarter than the average nineteen year old—I have an IQ over one forty and grades that had every Ivy League banging down my door last year—makes me wonder what college really has to offer me.

Nevertheless, my parents wouldn't hear of it. They had stressed the importance of a good education—even if the diploma did just collect dust on a shelf while I fed my hunger for adventure with a backpack and a compass *or whatever.* These were my parents' musings as they all but shoved me out the door. So, here I am, five hours from my parents' house, in an apartment smaller than my room at home, prepared to take on Camden Graf University, my next adventure. *College.*

I'm startled from my thoughts by a banging on the door and I approach it with caution, wondering who in the world would be looking for me. I know no one in D.C., and classes don't start for another two days. I know this is a building for students, but I thought I'd slid in sight unseen, opting for a Saturday morning move-in when I was sure more than half of the residents would be hungover from the night before.

I press my face to the door, standing on my tiptoes to peer out the peephole. "I'm not going to bite, open up! It's the building welcome wagon!" I see a girl with blonde hair wielding a bottle of champagne and a tray of brownies.

I open the door, but not too far, not wanting her to take it as an invitation to come in. To be honest, all I want to do is go to bed early, and a chatty neighbor that wants to stay up to the wee hours of the morning gabbing like girlfriends and trading life stories would definitely throw a wrench in that plan.

"Hey, neighbor!" The girl, who seems no older than me but certainly taller than me, stands in my entryway. A crop top barely covers her breasts, and high-waisted pants are cut off at her ankles, exposing her bare feet. Her blonde hair is pulled into a sleek ponytail secured at the back of her head, and a small diamond stud gleams from her nose. Her makeup looks like she's just stepped off a runway show, with perfect lashes and lipstick. "Welcome to the building. I'm Peyton. Peyton White. And you are?"

"Skyler," I tell her as she hands me the plate of brownies and begins to pour the *Andre* champagne into a solo cup.

Andre? But…why? There are so many better options than this toilet bubbly. I wrinkle my nose slightly and shake my head.

"Oh, what, you don't drink? Shit. I have some *La Croix* in my fridge."

My mouth waters; I do love *La Croix*. But I also love champagne. I just am not about to drink *that*.

Don't be a bitch, Sky. My sister's words blare in my head. "I drink. I just…haven't had much to eat, and I'm a bit of a lightweight." *Lie number one.*

"Oh! Well, have a brownie. Come on, a bunch of us are pregaming at my place to go out tonight. You should totally come."

"You know, tonight isn't great, I'm supposed to meet up with some old friends." I shake my head. *Lie number two.*

She raises an eyebrow at me as if she doesn't believe me. "Where ya from?"

"Connecticut."

"Really? Is it as boring as the stereotypes say?"

I take a tentative sip of the champagne she'd handed me and force myself not to gag. *God that's terrible.* "Yep. Pretty much."

"I'm from Seattle. Yes, it rains all the fucking time. No, I don't know Edward Cullen or Christian Grey or the people from *Grey's Anatomy*," she says as if she says that every time she tells someone where she's from.

I laugh at her joke. "I've never been to Seattle but it's on my list. I want to see the Space Needle and go to that market everyone talks about." I close my eyes, picturing the red letters in the sign.

"Pike Place? It's not *that* cool." She scrunches her nose in disgust as if she's just heard a terrible dad joke.

"Still, it's something renowned." I shrug.

"Fine, we can go or whatever."

And I almost choke on my drink as I hear the undertone of her comment. *We are besties now and you can come home with me for breaks!*

"Right, well, it was really nice to meet you, Peyton. I'm sure I'll see you around." I begin to shut the door when she stops it with her foot and hands me the bottle of champagne.

"I'm just right down the hall in 408 when you decide to stop being lame and pretending that you have anything to do tonight. I have tequila, and the starting lineup of the boy's soccer team." She gives me a wink. "Ciao, Bella!" She skips back to her apartment and flings open the door dramatically, letting the sounds of Kendrick Lamar float out into the hall.

I'm still momentarily speechless; having heard my native language thrown out there as well as the nickname my mother calls me. I know that non-Italians used the phrase often, but it still throws me whenever I hear it.

I look down at my arm again.

Life goes on, Bella.

I could either sit in this apartment and mope over *he who shall not be named* or I could embrace this new adventure, even if it isn't hiking in Santorini. It takes me about thirty seconds to come up with my decision before I take a swig from the bottle.

"Ugh! First things first, teach Peyton what decent champagne is."

I wrap the final strand of my newly highlighted hair around the wand before unplugging it from the wall in my tiny bathroom. There is barely enough room for me in here; heaven forbid I ever have a guy in here with me. My heart thumps and so does my sex. *I am not ready for that!* my heart tells me. *But I am!* my sex responds. The space between my legs has felt a dull hum ever since the words *boys soccer team* fell from Peyton's lips.

Well, at least I'm not totally broken.

I let out a sigh as I take in my reflection in the mirror.

Okay, Sky, Peyton is nice. Maybe at least try and make friends? It's time to let your guard down a little. Not everyone is going to screw you over like... my heart slams into my ribcage and my stomach turns. I'm not sure if it's from the champagne or the thoughts of walking in on my ex with some girl's legs wrapped around his face.

Ugh.

The white, off the shoulder top I'm wearing is the perfect contrast to my tan skin that I got *by nature,* not by bottle. Tucked into a pair of black shorts and sandals that tie up my leg, I'm not sure what look I'm going for exactly, but I look hot. My honey blonde hair that I had recently chopped off to shoulder length—spurred on by the words, "a woman who changes her hair is about to change her life"—bounces as I make my way down the hall. I have a clutch armed with the necessities in one hand and a bottle of vodka in the other. Sure, Peyton said they had alcohol, but I was taught to never show up anywhere empty handed.

I knock on the door and when it opens a billow of marijuana smoke floats out around me into the hallway. I wave a hand across my face. "Skyler! Sorry about that." Peyton waves the smoke away and drags me inside. "You came!"

"Yeah, uh...my friends flaked."

"Ugh, bitches! Well, I'm so glad you're here! Guys, guys!" She tries to quiet the noise and, while some of the guys turn their attention to her, most continue what they're doing. I notice although her apartment is about the same size as mine, it looks way bigger. She has a table pushed against the wall where four guys are playing beer pong. Shot glasses litter the bar in the kitchen as people play what I believe to be *Quarters*. There's an array of playing cards on her *IKEA* coffee table, and four people surrounding it as they try not to crack the beer in the center. "This is Skyler, my new neighbor. Everyone say hi!"

Most of them say hi and wave as if this was that bar where everyone knows your name. I smile, and wave back, slightly intimidated at being put on the spot. I'm not shy, far from it, but being around people I don't know, in an unfamiliar city, without so much as a wing woman or at the very least one person I know well, makes me a bit uneasy. I'm ashamed to admit I miss my mom, miss home, miss…I squeeze my eyes shut. *No, Sky.*

"Let's get you a drink, huh?"

"Oh, I brought something," I say as I hand her the Grey Goose.

"Oh fancy! I'm not wasting this on these assholes. You and I can drink this tomorrow in our mimosas," she says as I follow her into the kitchen.

"Mimosas have champagne…" It's more of a statement but it comes out like a question.

"You've never had them with vodka? Oh, girl, it'll change your life." She turns towards me and bounces on her toes like she's dying to share a secret with me.

"Isn't that just a screwdriver?" I feel like she's speaking an entirely different language that I'm not familiar with. I know alcohol, for the most part, having spent the majority of my senior year of high school—*and a few months in*

Italy—becoming well acquainted with the term "black-out" despite my under twenty-one status.

"Just trust me, alright? I'll hook ya up." And because on some level, I swear guys are pre-dispositioned to hear the words "hook" and "up" when used close together in a sentence, one manifests in front of us.

"P, who's your friend?" he asks as he slides a hand over her shoulder and points at me. I go through the *ManFax*—as my best friend, Stella, always says—as I survey the man in front of me. Tall. Blonde. No facial hair, but a cute face nonetheless. Muscular. Blue eyes. All American Boy.

"Skyler. Weren't you listening?" She pushes his arm off of her. "And no."

"No what?"

"No and no. Go away."

"Cockblock," he grumbles as he walks away, and I wonder if there is something going on between them.

"He's fucked ninety percent of the girls in this room. Yes, I fall into that ninety percent. Let's not dwell on it." She hands me a Jell-O shot. "Just...it's for the best. His dick game isn't even all that great. Which is why I have not been back for seconds," she says through a mouthful of the red gelatin that had far more *Everclear* vodka than was probably safe. "But he's hot."

Two hours later, more than half the party has left to hit the bars, armed with their fake IDs and willingness to make bad decisions. I sit on Peyton's bed as she rifles through her closet trying to come up with something to change into.

"What you have on is fine, Peyton. Shouldn't we go soon? It's getting late."

"Late? It's midnight. The only reason people left earlier is one of the bars offers a Power Hour between eleven and twelve which means half priced shots and mixed drinks. Trust me, it's still early." I hiccup as I take another sip of my drink when there's a beep from her nightstand. My eyes flit to the sound and she squeals with delight. "An OC notification! Yes!" She fist pumps the air and moves to her phone, her eyes lighting up with intrigue and excitement.

"O...C?" I ask, feeling the effects of the alcohol starting to catch up with me.

"Yeah, *Our Circle!* It's this new dating app!"

"Oh." I groan. "So, like *Tinder* or *Bumble* or whatever?" I'd never been on a dating app, but Stella swears by them. That girl goes on more first dates than anyone I know.

"Better!"

"They always are, right? Until something better comes along?" *There's always some new dating app that's supposedly better than the last. It's just the latest craze.*

"No, this really is better. You can only join if you're invited by someone else."

"Oh, so kind of like how Facebook started?"

"Right! Well, not anymore. My sister's unborn child has a Facebook already." Peyton rolls her eyes and holds her phone up for me to see the app.

"So, you get invited and then what? You get unsolicited dick pics by, not randoms necessarily, but by someone who knows someone who knows someone that may be your neighbor's cousin's ex-boyfriend?"

"It takes the element out of whether or not they're a psycho!"

"No...no, it doesn't." I chuckle as I listen to her backwards logic.

"Well...I haven't met any yet. All the guys I've met have been totally normal. And *gorgeous*. And smart. A lot of guys from the grad schools in the area are on here. Of course, I do have my age preferences set just a teensy bit higher."

"What's a teensy bit?" I ask, wondering if this girl is about to unleash her wealth of daddy issues on me.

"Just twenty-two to like…forty."

"FORTY? Peyton, how old are you?"

"Nineteen, relax."

"That's like…your dad's age."

"Well, I never knew my dad, so…Psych major me." She rolls her eyes as if she already knows what I'm going to say.

I hold my hands up as if to say *no judgment*. "I think I want to try it."

Her head snaps up from her phone and looks at me. "Really? I can invite you."

"Sure. Why not?"

"Atta girl! Okay, what's your Facebook name."

"Oh…" My face falls as I remember the social media disappearing act I'd done. "I deleted it."

"What?" She cocks her head to the side. "Why? And more importantly, how do you know when it's people's birthdays? I mean Instagram only goes so far. You do have Instagram, right?"

I nod. I wasn't sure how to tell this blonde bombshell that had probably never had her heart broken before that I deleted it so I didn't have to see my ex-boyfriend and his new girlfriend… excuse me, fiancée. He was the man *I* thought *I* was going to marry, the man that…*No, Skyler.*

I let out a breath. "A stupid boy."

"Ah, say no more. Okay, I think you can do it through your email. What is it?"

"Bella dot Mitchell at Gmail," I tell her and she looks at me curiously.

"Bella?"

"It's what my mom calls me. I'm Italian."

"Hot. Definitely put that in your profile. The guys were all salivating over you when you walked in by the way. I have six messages from guys here asking for your number and or 'deal.' Are you DTF?" she asks, and I wonder when we got to this level where she's comfortable enough to ask whether I'm down to fuck. I'm not a prude, but come on. I'd barely spoken two words to any of these guys that were allegedly asking.

"Ummm." I clear my throat. "Not…like right this second?" I wince.

"Oh, time of the month?" She blanches.

My face turns slightly pink, as if surfing the crimson wave was the only reason I may not want to have sex with a guy I just met. "No, I just…"

"Okay, so no, totally cool. The playing hard to get route. I love it. Okay, I sent you the link. Let's set up your profile before we leave, so you can get a feel for it while we're out. It's a Saturday night so it's a perfect time."

I had a feeling Peyton wouldn't take no for an answer, and I had a lot of vodka infused Jell-O in my stomach, coupled with two very strong vodka drinks that told me that this was probably a great idea. So, I let Peyton set up my profile, pulling pictures from my Instagram: one of me with my dog and a glass of wine, one of me in New York with Stella being embarrassing tourists on a ferry in front of the *Statue of Liberty*, one of me in a bathing suit, and finally one of me throwing a penny into the *Trevi Fountain*, a picture taken by…

"Oh, I bumped my age up a few years by the way. Do you want to? Guys our age are annoying."

I was no stranger to lying about my age. I had a fake ID, a really good one that put me at twenty-two. "Ummm. Well, what age did you put?"

"Twenty-two."

"Okay…sure, why not?"

"Okay, Sky—"

"Bella," I tell her. "Can you make my name Bella?"

"Skyler is a great name. You sure you don't want to use that?"

"It's also pretty uncommon. What if some psycho tracks me down?"

"Fine, *Bella*. What do you want in your profile? Def write that you're Italian. Can you speak it fluently?"

"I knew Italian before I knew English. Yeah." I chuckle thinking about how my father spoke only English while my mother spoke to me in Italian growing up.

"Okay how about this: New to the area by way of Italy. Name isn't actually Bella." She looks up from my phone. "Give me a fun fact."

"Ummm. I love iced coffee?"

"What girl doesn't? Next."

"Okay, ummm, I have a tattoo that—"

"Really? Tattoos and iced coffee? Groundbreaking." She rolls her eyes and I swear to God it's like I can hear my sister's voice.

"I was going to say, just put the quote I have on my arm, smartass." I point to my arm and she squints, probably because her vision is a bit blurry.

"What's it say?"

"La vita va avanti."

"English?"

"Life goes on."

"It's not exactly the vibe you want for a dating app. Sounds a bit morose if you ask me."

"It's not! It's supposed to be inspiring and motivating. The kick in the ass you need just when you need it."

Her lips form a straight line. "Aaaaaand, iced coffee it is."

With Peyton's arm locked through mine, we walk down the sidewalk with a few people behind us. My phone had been buzzing ever since she made the profile, mostly *heys* and *what are you up to tonight?* and *where's the party?* A few guys tried to banter with me in Italian but I lost interest the second I realized they were using Google translate. *That shit is never accurate.*

This isn't quite like those apps where you had to "like" each other to communicate. No, this served kind of like a chat room, where everyone within the radius you permitted could message you. You could reject the chat or block, and only once you accepted did it reveal your bio. It didn't seem one hundred percent safe or effective, but Peyton insisted that they were just working out the kinks.

Sheesh, with the way she advocated for this app, you'd think she created it.

A picture of a man flashes across my screen and I almost drop my phone because holy mother fuck is he gorgeous. *Aidan.* The first thing that captivates me are his eyes. They're the most fascinating shade of aquamarine. Not quite blue, not quite green. I'd never seen that color as someone's iris before. The Caribbean waters, yes. But someone's eyes? *Never.* His dark brown hair looks as if he'd spent the time just before the picture was taken, pulling on it. His sideburns connect to some sexy facial hair all across his jaw, and his perfect, straight teeth almost blind me. He stares at the camera, standing with two other guys that look like they probably share DNA. In his second picture he's in a cap and gown, for what looks like his Doctorate, and Ray Bans cover his face that makes me weak in the knees. The final picture he's standing on top of a mountain, holding his hands out with that stunning smile. I take note of his very muscular arms trapped beneath his t-shirt.

I accept his chat request immediately, desperate to know more about this gorgeous creature.

"Oh, he's hot as fuck! How come he's never shown up on mine before? What's his bio say?" Peyton leans over my shoulder as we stop walking to read what it says.

"New to DC. Where the fuck is there to hike around here? Will give you tacos and/or mimosas if you tell me. Bonus if I can convince you to come. Oh, and I'm taller than you."

"I love hiking!" I shriek.

"Ew, why?" Peyton blanches as we start walking towards the bars again. "Message him!"

"What do I say?"

"Oh God, Sky. Tell me you know how to flirt with boys. You're not a virgin, right? Ohmigod." She stops. "Did I throw you into the lion's den with no way to tame the beasts?" Her eyes are wide and unblinking.

"No, no, no." I shake my head. "Not a virgin. Just, I've never really used an app before, and I'm not witty in text."

"Everyone is witty in text…okay, that's not true. But girls are better because we usually discuss the replies as a group. Okay," she rambles, "make it easy. It says he's new to DC, ask where he's from!"

"Oh, that's good." I nod as I type out a message.

Bella: Fellow newbie! Where are you from?

Peyton groans next to me. "Did I tell you to say all of that? God, you're a dork."

I frown and look down at my message brought on by definitely too much alcohol. "Should I add a smiley?"

"No girl, chill."

Aidan: Hey Bella, I'm from Boston. And you're gorgeous. Just needed to put that out there.

"OH, we are so in there!" Peyton giggles. "Fuck tonight, let's go back to my place and sext your new boyfriend."

"I don't think it's a two person job, and no one is sexting anyone! He said I was pretty—"

"Gorgeous. He used the word gorgeous, Skyler. Now reply. Tell him you want to sit on his hot face."

"I am not saying that."

"Fiiiiine, or thank you." She shrugs. "Whatever." My phone pings again.

Aidan: Too fast. Sorry. So, you're really from Italy? Or you're Italian?

Bella: No not fast! Thank you, and I'm Italian but I'm from Connecticut.

Aidan: What brings you to DC?

I start to type out school but then I remember I'm supposed to be twenty-two. "I always go with grad school," Peyton interjects. "And I never say CGU."

"Right."

Bella: Just moved here for school.

Aidan: Nice! Where are you going?

I glance at Peyton and she rolls her eyes. "Just say Georgetown. Guys cream their panties over a smart girl."

"I am a smart girl," I retort.

"Oh, perfect!"

"We go to CGU, of course we're smart." CGU is like the less pretentious version of Georgetown. You need the grades or the legacy to get in here, and I have both.

"Eh, my parents donated like four libraries here. My GPA did not do anything for me, and I was stoned during my SATs. I think I guessed B for like every question." She shrugs and I giggle. *This girl is growing on me.*

I didn't like the idea of outright lying to him though.

Bella: I don't have my real name on this app and you think I'm just going to hand up my school on a platter? What if you're a serial killer?

Aidan: Fair. But I am not a serial killer.

Bella: Right like you'd tell me. *eye roll emoji*

Aidan: Ha. What's your real name anyway? Or can I not know that either?

Bella: Maybe one day.

Aidan: Bella means beautiful in Italian, right? I would say that it's fitting.

"Okay in like five minutes he's called you gorgeous and beautiful. He totes wants in your panties." Peyton claps her hands and squeals.

I want him in my panties too, God damn!

We approach the bar and the bouncer lets us in without so much as a glance at my ID. I wonder if I actually look twenty-one as he stamps my hand and ushers us inside. We've lost most of Peyton's friends, having stopped to thoroughly stalk Aidan's profile. I go to reply to his message when I see another one has come through.

Aidan: What are you doing tonight? Do you want to meet up?

My breath catches in my throat seeing his words on the screen. *Am I ready for this? Casual sex? We certainly aren't meeting up at midnight to just talk.*

"What he say, what he say?" Peyton asks, and when I look up she's holding a shot of some amber colored liquid to her lips and holding one out for me.

"What's that?" I ask her as I hold it under my nose. I'm immediately flooded with a sense of nostalgia.

"Fireball, duh."

"Right. Okay." I take the shot, letting the cinnamon flavored whiskey slide down my throat tasting like bad decisions and regret. "He asked if I wanted to meet up."

"Ummm duh. Ask where he is! Ask if he has friends with him. A good fuck always clears my head and God knows I am not ready for Physics 101 on Monday morning."

I take a deep breath, letting the alcohol lower my inhibitions.

Why not?

Bella: I'm at Lush. Where are you?

Aidan

"*Oh shit, dude she replied! No thanks to you* acting like a fucking thirsty ass." My buddy Chace says as he holds up my phone he'd stolen from me to stop me from acting like, as he so eloquently put it, *a thirsty ass*. "In five messages, you told her she was gorgeous and beautiful. Might as well have just asked her if you could fuck a baby into her."

We sit at the somewhat crowded bar where there seems to be a shortage of women. It makes me wonder what the hell Chace was thinking suggesting we stay here when he thinks with his dick ninety-nine percent of the time. "I wouldn't say that."

"You don't have to. You reek of desperation and *I'm ready to get married and start a family* vibes."

"Women love that."

"Not twenty-two year old, hot Italians that have a bikini pic on a dating profile. Join *Match* or I don't know, *Christian Mingle* for that shit."

"I didn't want to join this in the first place. You invited me, took my phone and created my profile all in the span of a shower. Why'd I even invite you here for the weekend?" I groan. I had stupidly thought that having my best friend here my second weekend in D.C. would make this transition easier. After the nasty break up with my now ex-fiancée that resulted in her breaking half of my stuff and kicking me out of the apartment we'd bought together, this teaching job at CGU couldn't have come at a better time.

"You need to get out there. You've been fucking what—like one girl the past four years?" An incredulous look finds his face as if he can't fathom the thought.

"Well yeah, that's kind of what being in a committed relationship means."

"Monogamy is for the fuckin birds." He sighs as he rubs the heel of his hand into his eye.

"You just haven't met the right woman," I tell him as I down the rest of my beer with an ABV that is close to pushing me into dangerous territory.

Do not fucking call Corinne.

"And evidently neither have you." He swings his eyes towards me. "Or I'm sorry, you and Corinne...?" He narrows his eyes curiously as if he'd missed the last few months. Missed me moping around like a sorry asshole as I mourned the last four years of my life. Years I spent with a manipulative bitch that was undoubtedly the best sex I'd ever had. With a woman who, despite her flaws, had gotten in deep and made me fall in love with her. With her chestnut brown hair and icy blue eyes that could get me to do just about anything. *Fuck, I miss her.*

NO.

"Fuck off, Chace. Is this you helping?"

"I'm here for tough love. If you're looking for someone to throw you a pity party, call your sister or maybe James. But this ain't my lane." My sister Beth was still in Boston currently dating my other best friend James. I'm not going to say I have a problem with it, but I'm not going to say I don't either. *That asshole better watch his back.*

"I'm here to get you laid," he continues. "Or at the very least a blow job. Because frankly, dude, you need it. How long has it been anyway? Like seven months?"

"We've only been broken up for three."

"My question still stands. James said y'all stopped fucking months before you broke up."

"God, you guys gossip like girls, I swear to fuck."

Chace holds his hand up and motions for the bartender. "We are losing focus. I need to reply to hot Bella."

"Don't call her that," I growl, and for some reason it does piss me off. Maybe because I'm thinking once we get there, I'll pussy out and Chace will end up taking Bella home. *Well, not back to my apartment. Fuck that.*

I find myself wondering where Bella lives and a part of me hopes that she lives alone in case things were to escalate to a private party.

"Testy." He hands the bartender—a woman that for some reason Chace *isn't* making eyes at—his credit card.

"Thanks," I tell him as he pays for our drinks. "You're not into the bartender? She seems like your type?" Strands of thick jet black hair fall from her bun and dance along her mocha skin. She's stacked like a fucking supermodel, complete with curves that you only saw on a select blessed few. Her full lips, that have a hint of pink, quirk up, revealing a deep dimple whenever Chace talks to her.

"*Girl* is my type. But your obsession with monogamy didn't peep the ring on her finger?"

"Oh...I guess not." I rub my face, scratching the facial hair. "Thought it wouldn't stop you from flirting though."

"I don't believe in going to a buffet if I can't eat." He looks at me and then back to the bartender who is heading our way with his card and receipt. "Can we focus? Are we going to *Lush* or nah? It sure beats the hell out of this place." He looks around at the bar that is clearing out by the second.

The bartender sets the receipt down and the dimple pops out in full force. "I get cut in twenty." She smiles and Chace raises an eyebrow at her.

"As flattered as I am, I don't do other guys' girls." He points to the band on her left ring finger.

She flexes her left hand. "I'm not married. Or engaged. Or seeing anyone. I wear it on this hand to keep guys from hitting on me. It works like twelve percent of the time." She rolls her eyes before she leans forward. "Usually on the guys that I *want* to hit on me." A giggle leaves her lips and I watch as Chace shifts in his seat. I can already see how this is going to go down.

"Care to come with us to *Lush*? I'm playing wingman for my boy here." He wraps an arm around my neck and I shake my head.

"I never said we were going."

He lets me go and nudges my shoulder. "You asked her to meet up!"

"No. *You* asked her to meet up," I correct him with a scowl.

"Tomato tomahto. It's your name and your face. Don't ghost her. She's cute." I go to protest when he beats me to it. "I never said she wasn't gorgeous or beautiful, I said you didn't need to tell *her* that."

I huff. "Fine. Tell her we're coming. *I'm* coming." I look over to see that Chace is already typing out a message. He hands my phone back to me and I roll my eyes.

Aidan: Be there in twenty. I'm coming with a few friends. I hope you like tequila.

"*I* don't even like tequila." I look up from the message he sent her.

"And that's a problem in itself. Man the fuck up."

"The last time I had tequila I woke up forty minutes from my apartment in a sombrero and my underwear." I grimace at both the memory and the horror of that Uber ride home.

"Ah, Cinco de Mayo 2017, good times." He nods as he remembers.

I scowl at him, remembering the only reason he wasn't right next to me where he belonged, when it was *his* idea to go to a party on the other side of town at 2 AM, was because *of course*, he had met a girl. "I'm not drinking tequila."

"Oh, well this is awkward." The bartender smiles as she sets two shot glasses of a clear liquid in front of me and Chace.

Chace's eyes light up and he grins. "Oh God, I think I just fell in love. What's your name again?"

"Taryn. Now drink up, buttercups. If we're going to *Lush*, you're going to want to be drunk. Trust me." She points between the two glasses as she wipes down the bar around us and heads back to the other side.

"I hate you *so* much right now."

"What, because my good looks and charm got us free tequila shots?"

"No, because you're hell bent on ruining my life."

"Don't be so dramatic. Do you want to be stiff and awkward around Bella?"

"No. Well…wait, I'm not stiff or awkward."

"I am not even going to dignify that with a response," Chace says before he downs the shot. "Oh, and the good stuff too. It'll go down like water. Trust me." He nods at my shot. "Come on, buttercup. Bottoms up."

"Fuck you."

"Hey, if I swung that way, I'd totally help ya out. God knows you need it to help pry that stick out of there."

Taryn leads us towards *Lush,* and I'll admit I actually like her. Perhaps if Chace doesn't fuck things up with her by acting like a complete dick we could be friends or whatever. She gives Chace her fair share of sass and I can tell that he's enjoying keeping up with her.

"Here we are!" She shimmies as she goes to the front of the line, bypassing the line of people down the block.

"Umm…" I start when Chace gives me a warning look telling me to shut up.

"Hey, Kyle." Taryn high fives the bouncer and points over her shoulder at us. "I've got some D.C. bar virgins. Let me in!"

"I am the furthest thing from a virgin." Chace wraps a hand around her and tugs on a lock of her hair that she's long released from the confines of her bun, while growling in her ear. I roll my eyes at his innuendo as Kyle waves us in.

The bar is dark; the only light in the hallway is from my phone as I stare down at Bella's last message.

Bella: Okay! Let me know when you're here! *smiley face*

I have to admit I was glad that Chace forced me to come here. Maybe he was right. A night with a gorgeous woman underneath me screaming out my name may be just what I need.

Despite my lack of sex towards the end with Corinne, I did know what I was doing in bed. And before Corinne, I had a very good track record of making women come. *Corinne was just a frigid bitch.*

EXACTLY.

Aidan: Just got here, where are you?

We push through another set of doors and it's significantly lighter. I suddenly feel like I've stepped through the door to my past. At thirty-two, I'm definitely the oldest person here. *Holy fuck.*

"Told ya you needed to be drunk," Taryn says as she takes in my expression. Chace, who is the same age as me, is probably salivating and also regretting that he'd RSVP'd to this college girl party with a plus one.

"Wow, is there anyone here over the age of twenty-one?"

"This is the college bar. A lot of CGU kids," she informs me as I follow behind her and Chace towards the bar.

Great. Just what I need, running into a future student of mine. I let out a breath, relieved that I only had one person in mind to talk to tonight and she was a twenty-two year old grad student. She's still a bit young, but at least I don't have to worry about her being in here with a fake, *or* being in my Monday morning Social Justice lecture.

Taryn orders our beers and Chace all but knocks her hand out of the way when she tries to pay, shooting her a warning glare, and she raises her hands in defeat. "So, where's Bella?" she asks as Chace pays for our drinks.

"No idea, I asked and she hasn't replied."

"Well, look for a short, tan, blonde-ish girl." Chace takes a sip of his drink and looks around the room. He's a few inches over six feet like me, but has me by an inch something that he never lets me forget.

I'm in the process of scanning the room for Bella when I hear a shrill voice from a few feet away over the music thumping through the speakers. "Four shots of fireball!" I turn slightly to see a blonde girl in a crop top leaning over the bar as she shakes her ass to the beat slightly. *I am way too old to be here.*

The girl in question must have felt my gaze because she peeks over her shoulder and her eyes light up. I'm used to that look, and although she's cute, she isn't exactly my type. The tequila shot from earlier, mixed with all of the other drinks I've had, has me thinking that I want to at least meet Bella and see that gorgeous smile.

And okay maybe more than that. I mean she is pretty fuckable.

I give her a tight smile when her hand finds my bicep. "You're the hottie from Boston!"

"That's usually my nickname," Chace interjects and looks at me as if to say, *Who's this?*

She giggles and bounces on her heels. "Oh my God, Wes totally owes me twenty bucks. He said you catfished Sky."

I shake my head completely at a loss at what the fuck she's talking about. "Catfished?"

"It means pretending to be someone else on the internet. Watch TV dude," Chace says.

"Oh. Um. No," I tell her, as I look down at the hand she still has on my arm.

"Come on. We have a table."

"Oh, I'm meeting someone—"

"Yes, I know. Skyler." She puts her hands on her hips and looks behind me at Chace and Taryn. "When you said you were bringing friends, I was hoping they'd be *single* guys. God, really!?" She rolls her eyes. "Oh, I'm Peyton."

"Peyton. I'm sorry, but I'm so lost. And a little drunk. So speak…not girl."

She purses her lips and then her eyes seem to focus slightly and she slaps a hand over her head. "Oh! Right, alias name or whatever. Skyler is Bella. That's her real name. The girl you're talking to on OC. Also, you're welcome, because she wanted to stay in tonight and like sleep or whatever." She starts walking away and I follow slowly behind her with Chace and Taryn behind me.

"Is she for real?" I hear Chace whisper. "She's hot as fuck though."

"Aren't you…" I shoot him a look, my eyebrow quirked at him as I think about Taryn who is following behind us. I know she didn't hear him, what with her being a good foot shorter than us both, but *damn Chace.*

"I'm just sayin'."

We make it through a throng of people and it's as if my body senses her before I see her. As we approach the table I see she's seated with one other girl and two other guys, bottles and glasses stacked along the table. I watch her suck a lime between her lips, her eyes squeezed shut as she cringes slightly.

"Whew, that was bad." She shivers slightly as she opens her eyes and drops the lime in the empty shot glass. Her brown eyes find mine instantly and for a moment it feels like no one else is there—certainly not the guy that seems to be seated just a little too close to her.

"Look who I found!" her friend cheers, and Bella—Skyler—stands. I'm taken aback both by how stunning she is and how short she is. *Fuck.* Visions of fucking her petite body against the wall move to the forefront of my brain and I begin running through the states and capitals, Bill of Rights, periodic table of elements. Something. *Anything*—that would will my dick down faster as she moves towards me. Her teeth are pushed into her bottom lip and *that is definitely not helping.* "Aidan!" She smiles. "Holy shit, you're so tall!" My eyes roam down her body and I notice she's in flats but she's standing almost on her tippy toes…to get closer to me, I assume.

I don't know what's gotten into me or what prompts me to do it, but before I can think I have her in my arms, my large body engulfing her tiny one in a hug and lifting her slightly off the ground. I press my face into her neck inhaling her sweet scent. "Bella," I whisper in her ear and she shivers again. I'm pleased that this has nothing to do with a bad shot. I set her down and give her a smirk. "I mean, Skyler?"

She nods before shooting a look at Peyton who's staring at us like we're her only source of entertainment with a dreamy look on her face.

"My mom calls me Bella."

"I like Skyler," I tell her honestly. It suits her.

A hint of pink finds her cheeks. "Thank you. I'll pass your praise off to my parents." Her lips quirk up.

Her vibe is infectious and I find myself smiling as well. "Can I buy you a drink?" I ask her, wanting nothing more than to get away from the prying eyes that are watching our interaction.

I feel a hand around my neck and I groan inwardly remembering I didn't come alone. "My friend has no manners. I'm Chace." He smiles at her and she nods.

"Hi, it's nice to meet you." She holds her hand out and I'm pleased that she doesn't try to hug him even if I do think she's friendly.

He looks at me. "Dude, I think we're going to take off." He looks back at Skyler. "Little lady, I assume you can make sure my friend gets home safely?" He raises an eyebrow at her and she giggles.

"Yes, of course." She nods. "I've only been in D.C. twelve hours though. I basically only know where this bar is and my apartment."

"Well, I didn't say *which* home." He grins and I resist the urge to punch him. *Can you not make me come off like I'm a complete fuckboy?*

"Okay, bye, Chace." I push him away and nod at Taryn.

"Text me if you're coming home tonight," he whispers in my ear before he disappears.

I'm left alone with Skyler and her friends, and I have to admit I only feel a little bit awkward. They look young as well, but I guess twenty-two really is ten years younger than me.

I manage to catch the look Skyler gives Peyton before she turns to me. And if my assumption is correct, she's pleased with how the evening has played out so far. "Let's go get that drink."

Skyler

H*OLY FUCKING SHIT. MY CLIT IS ON FIRE.*

This has never happened before. Never have I had such a strong reaction to a man, not to mention a complete stranger. My heart is racing and the thump in my sex is getting more aggressive as Aidan's large, warm hand squeezes mine. He pulls me through a crowd of people sweating and grinding to the beat of the familiar Rihanna song that blares through the speakers. We make it to the bar and when he turns to face me, he takes my breath away leaving me truly speechless. My neck is almost completely tilted back because he's *that fucking tall. God damn, I could climb him like a tree!* My gaze moves down his perfectly chiseled face to his mouth, and perfectly shaped lips I'm dying to suck on. I see his lips moving but I can't make out what he's saying over the roar of the crowd and the even louder one between my legs. I swallow when I notice his lips stop moving. "What?" I cock my head and put a finger behind my ear, letting him know I couldn't hear him. When he leans down I feel his breath, hot and cool at the same time, and it sends a shiver down my spine. "What are you drinking?"

"Oh. Ummm. Whatever." I try to shoot him my best *I'm laid back and totally chill and absolutely not freaking out about how fine you are and trying my best not to make a fool of myself* look. "How about a shot? I think I'm feeling frisky." My teeth graze my bottom lip and, despite the dim lighting, I notice his jaw tick slightly and his Adam's apple wobbles.

He nods once. "One shot coming up. Any preference?"

"Surprise me."

He turns around and I take the time to admire his backside. I cock my head slowly to the side, *wishing* I had X-ray vision to see the ass I'm fantasizing about biting, licking, and dragging my nails across as he plows into me. My phone vibrates in my hand and I look down.

> **Peyton: I'll take my thank you in the form of breakfast tomorrow, please! I take my coffee black like my soul.**
>
> **Me: He is SO hot! Holy shit.**
>
> **Peyton: Agreed! Sucks his very fuckable friend brought a girl with him though.**
>
> **Me: You think Chace is hot?**

I try to recall the *ManFax* on Chace. *Hmm.* I remember tall, and muscles bulging under a white t-shirt, and jeans. And a backwards hat. Oh and a smile that probably made women drop their panties on sight. But I was too busy trying to keep my panties up around Aidan to really notice.

> **Me: Sorry about that! I figured he would have brought someone single.**
>
> **Peyton: No worries, there will be plenty of time for you to play wingman for me! How is he?**

Me: Nice. It's really loud though, we haven't talked much.

Peyton: Why are you talking at all? Go find a dark corner and make out! Or... get it on if you like a risk.

Me: In public?! Peyton, please. I am a lady! Haha

Peyton: With a man like that you better learn how to get UNladylike and QUICK. God, I would do very dirty things to a man like that.

Me: Hey!

Peyton: I'm just saying. Please tell me all the deets tomorrow. *smiley face*

I look up to find Aidan staring down at me, a smile tugging at his lips as he holds up a tiny plastic cup filled to the brim with a cloudy liquid.

"Did you roofie this?" I narrow my eyes at him and he shakes his head. A playful scolding look in his eyes makes me giggle. "It's cloudy."

"It's a lemon drop."

"Oh. Are they good? I don't think I've ever had one."

"They're alright. All of the alcohol here is garbage. Next time, we go to a bar that has something above Tito's vodka."

I wrinkle my nose, grateful that he seems to be a bit of an alcohol snob too. "Right? Most bars at least have Kettle One."

"Apparently this is a bar where a lot of the college kids hang out." We down our shots and I'm grateful to have a reason to ignore that comment given he doesn't know I'm one of *these* college kids. He sets the empty glasses on the counter before leading me towards a corner of the room. "Do you want to dance?" he asks.

I turn my head to look at the group of people on the dance floor before turning back to him.

"As much as I love to dance," I shake my head, "that's not what I'm really interested in doing right now." My head feels slightly fuzzy, the effects of the alcohol catching up with me and lowering my inhibitions even more.

"What do you want to do?" he asks as he tugs me towards a row of stools underneath a table facing the windows. He sits on a bar stool and as I go to sit beside him, he pulls me towards him, positioning me between his legs. "Or should I tell you what I'd like to do?"

The way he's looking at me, I can read it all over his face. His eyes are darker than the blue I saw in the app, almost navy, and it makes me wonder if there is some truth to eyes becoming darker when a person is aroused. His lips are parted slightly and I see his tongue peeking out slightly between his perfect teeth. I can feel his breath on my face as I move slightly closer, my body warm and tingly all over with the anticipation of what's to come.

"And what's that?" I ask.

"I want to kiss you." I lick my lips on instinct and a lascivious grin finds his lips. "Not those lips." I immediately feel my cheeks heat up but I smile in spite of my slight embarrassment at his words. He stands up, towering over me, but leans down and presses his lips to my ear. "I want to pin you to the wall and drive my cock inside of you until you don't know your own name." He hasn't touched me at this point, which makes this monologue even more arousing. I'm dying for him to touch me. Touch my pussy, my tits, my face. *Anything*. "I want to bend you over and eat your pussy until you cream all over my tongue. I bet you are so pretty when you come. I bet you lose control of your senses for a second, your eyes water and stream down your beautiful face because for a moment you're sure you saw God or whatever deity you believe in. Your toes curl, your legs are taut, your hands dig into whatever they can, as you try to tether yourself from floating away… I want to witness that while I have you underneath me." He pulls back and looks at me, waiting for my reply.

Moisture pools in my panties and I try my best to rub my legs together, praying I can graze the seam of my shorts and feel just a slight bit of friction against my sex. I clench and let out a breath as I look away from his penetrating gaze. I turn back to him. "I've never—had…"

"You've never had an orgasm?"

"No. I mean, yes! Just not one like…*that*." I'd had orgasms before. Self-inflicted of course. *And my ex…*My heart thumps, though I'll admit the intensity isn't as great as it used to be. He'd given me a few in our three months together, mostly with his tongue. I'd had sex with exactly two people and had yet to get off with a dick. And they were never soul-shattering, *I saw God* orgasms. Yet, something told me Aidan would probably change that. *I was in.*

"It's because I haven't fucked you yet."

I don't know if it's the alcohol, or my raging hormones, or the fact that he might be the most gorgeous man I've ever laid eyes on, but I'm in his arms before I know it. I tug on his black t-shirt, bringing him down to me, and planting my lips on his. It doesn't take but a second for us to find our rhythm. His tongue darts out of his mouth into mine and he groans the second ours meet. His hands are in my hair, mine are on his biceps, as I can't even reach the area behind his neck. I drag my hands down his chest, pressing my nails into the fabric and feeling the hard ridges of his chest. Every time I feel an ab my clit twitches.

"Come home with me," I blurt out, not wanting to wait another second without seeing what he can do with me, my body, my…pussy.

His lips quirk up into a smile, making me believe for the first time that there was something to the phrase *panty dropping grin*. "Let's go." He doesn't say another word as he pulls me from the bar, my short legs struggling to keep up with his longer ones.

I shoot a text to Peyton, telling her I'm leaving to have very hot sex with the very hot man from OC, and she replies with a string of emojis including a thumbs up, an eggplant, and a kissy face.

We settle into comfortable silence, his hand squeezing mine every few feet.

"Do you have condoms?"

He stops in his tracks and looks at me before an expression of realization dawns on him. "Fuck. At my apartment. Not on me. I didn't think when I came out tonight..." His eyes scan the road. "There has to be a convenience store or something around."

"Or we could just not..." I start and he actually growls at me.

"If I get you in a bed, I am not leaving it until my dick has been inside of you." I swallow hard and he closes the space between us. "Isn't that what you want? Or did I misread something?" His eyes scan my face, and lines of worry cross his.

I reach up and touch his face, stroking the slight stubble on his jaw. "No, I want it. But I... we could do other stuff... and then...another time..."

"My dick. Your pussy, Skyler. *Tonight.*"

A man had never talked to me like that before and the way my body hummed in response, *I think I liked it.*

"There's a convenience store slightly past my building."

"Come." He grabs my hand and pulls me along. I'm

shocked I don't feel more buzzed from the alcohol. Perhaps the buzz of my hormones is overpowering it.

It's a ten-minute walk to my building and when I point it out he stops. "Do you want to go up and I'll go get them?" I do a quick run through of my legs, underarms, and pussy. Everything is clean shaven and fresh. *Oh, but what state did I leave my apartment in?* I have some neuroses, so my apartment is pretty put together even though I just moved in this morning, but I can't remember if I'd left any CGU stuff out. *Maybe I should do a quick survey and light a few candles. And maybe change my panties. These are soaked.*

"Okay, yeah. I'll go up. Text me when you're back and I'll buzz you in?"

"Okay." He leans down and presses a kiss to my lips. "Don't change your underwear. I know they're wet, and I want a taste."

I nod as I try my best not to blush, not knowing what to say. I'm honestly more worried if I speak, the response, *"Okay, Daddy"* will fall from my lips.

Once I'm inside I let out a breath and am on the move, darting up the four flights of stairs, knowing that I don't have the patience for my elevator. My phone is pushed to my ear before I can even make it to my door. "Stels, wake up. Wake up!"

"What the fuck, do you know what time it is?" I hear groaned into the phone and I pull my phone away from my ear because I'm actually not sure. 2:14 AM my phone reads.

"Stella, oh my God. OH MY GOD!"

"Are you dying?"

"No."

"Hurt?"

"No, Stel, listen!"

"Then call me back at an appropriate hour, I have to work early in the morning. You know the brunch rush at the restaurant sucks." I straighten my bed, breathing a sigh of relief that I had in fact made it earlier. I throw a few stray clothes I had tossed on it while I was deciding what to wear earlier in a hamper before doing a quick inventory of any CGU stuff—given that he thinks I'm four years older than I am and definitely *not* in undergrad. Once I've successfully hidden everything, I dart into the bathroom to see its state. I toss my curling wand and makeup into a bin under the sink and straighten my shower curtain.

"Stella, I'm about to fuck the most BEAUTIFUL man I've ever met."

I hear some shuffling and then a throat clearing. "Okay, you have my attention." Her voice is firmer and I can already picture her sitting up in bed, grabbing her glasses from the nightstand and pushing them onto her face. "Where'd you meet him?"

"On this app called *Our Circle* or something? We matched and—"

"Jesus, Sky, you've been in D.C., what, five minutes?"

"Okay wrangle in that tone, Judge Judy," I tell her as I rummage through the drawer I threw my lighter in. I run through my apartment lighting every candle in sight. "I'll screenshot you a pic, but he's so fine. Like unbelievably gorgeous." I think about opening a bottle of wine but decide against it, thinking that Aidan didn't seem to have any plans to drink anything except for *me*.

"You said that already. Where is he anyway, as flattered as I am that you called to give me a play by play, tell me you didn't hide out in your bathroom to call me?"

"No, he went to get condoms."

"Oh man! So, I guess we're totally over Gabriel then?" I smell under my arms and rush back into the bathroom, swiping some deodorant under them, and spritzing myself with more of my *Prada* perfume. *Shit, should I change?*

"NAME!" I run into my room, toss the phone on the bed, and pull off the top I've been wearing. I replace it with a tanktop that exposes far more skin, as well as the lace of my bra that peeks out over the top.

"Oh right, he who shall not be named. My mistake."

"I don't know. Yes. No. Maybe? But…he's not an option. I have to move on." *Should I take my shorts completely off? Maybe I should just answer the door naked.*

Is that doing too much?

"Yes, I know, *la vita va avanti*," she says in an awful Italian accent.

My phone pings and when I pull my phone away I see the OC notification. I slap my forehead realizing he didn't actually have my number. "Stel, I'll call you tomorrow. He's back and I have to go have life changing sex with this hot man from Boston."

"Ooh Boston! Ask him if he 'parks his car in Harvard yard'?" she says with a horrible Boston accent and I roll my eyes.

"Bye, Stel."

"Toodles."

I open up the app and see his message.

Aidan: I'm here. Let me up, beautiful.

I swoon, just like I did the other two times he said it. If things never go past tonight, I'll never forget how this man treated me. How he made me feel from even the first message.

My heart thumps in my chest as I press the buzzer to let him up.

A few minutes later, I hear a knock at my door and I don't hesitate to open it, but I'm surprised to see him staring at me with a frown on his face. "Did you look?" He points at the peephole and I blush slightly.

"I knew it was you."

"Someone could have beat me up here. Or been lurking in your hallway."

"My building is safe, you have to be buzzed in," I tell him as he passes by me and crosses his arms as I shut the door and lock it.

When I turn around he's in front of me, boxing me against the door. "Look next time. Or I'll stand outside your door and vet all your guests. This isn't Connecticut, Princess."

Now, under normal circumstances, I'd bite the head off of any jerk who thought they could get away with that condescending comment and equally terrible pet name. But I can't stop myself from reacting to it. I can almost feel the cum leaking from my pussy into my panties. I nod. "Okay."

"Good girl." He presses his thumb to my chin before rubbing it across my lip.

"Do you want a tour?"

"Of your body?"

I giggle and shake my head. "My apartment." I walk by him. "Are you hungry or thirsty or..." I don't have a chance to finish when I'm lifted into his arms and his hands go under my butt. "You changed your top, giving me a delicious view of these perky tits, and you're asking me if I'm hungry for *food?*" He sets me on the counter and leans between my legs. "You and I both know I'm only interested in eating one thing."

I let out a breath. "Let's go to my bedroom."

His tongue darts out and licks his lips before he leans forward and drags his tongue from the space between my breasts, up my chest, neck, tracing the shell of my ear before he finds my mouth. "Holy shit," I murmur as he hauls me off the counter as if I weigh nothing and carries me through my apartment.

"I am going to devour you, Skyler," he whispers in my ear as he makes it to my room. There's a glow from the candles illuminating the room as he drops me on my bed and pulls his shirt off in a matter of seconds. "From the moment I saw you…fuck, baby." He presses his lips to my chest. *"Mi fai eccitare,"* he whispers and my eyebrows almost fly off my face as I hear his words in the perfect accent. *You turn me on.*

"You know…you know Italian?"

"I spent a semester abroad in undergrad, and then I went again in grad school. I love Italy."

"Oh my God. Say something else."

He chuckles as he undoes my shorts and pulls them torturously slow down my legs. *"Sei bellissima."* This man just told me I'm beautiful in Italian. *Holy fuck. Do not tell Mama.* She'll be planning our wedding before the end of the week.

My thoughts are halted as I feel him push his nose to my sex. "You didn't change them." He looks up from between my legs. "These are soaked." He presses his fingers into me, rubbing the lace of the fabric against my clit.

"I…" I shut my eyes. "I'm going to come."

"Already? Baby, we're just getting started."

"I'm a little…wound up."

He slides my panties down my legs and rubs them in his hands before pressing his nose to the wet fabric. "I'm going to keep these. Do you mind?"

"N—no," I stammer. I'd seen it in movies, read erotic

novels where the guy took her panties home but it'd never happened to me. *Maybe because you've only fucked two boys and this is so clearly a **man**.*

"Would a kiss take the edge off? A little kiss to your pretty pussy to ease the ache? Tell me what would make you feel better."

I squirm under his gaze. "Touch me, Aidan, please."

He stands up and pulls his pants down, revealing grey boxers and a darker spot making me smile that I've turned *him* on as much as he turns me on. "Do I get to keep those?" I point at them. "You know since you get mine?"

He smiles as he moves up the bed, his body flexing with each move. "I suppose that would be fair."

His hands find my sides raising my tank-top over my head and tossing it behind me. His eyes find my chest, and his hands palm my breasts gently as he presses his lips to mine. I part my naked legs, inviting him in between them and within no time, he's nestled into the space, his cock covered by the briefs that would soon belong to me. His hard member is nestled between the lips of my sex and he moves slightly bumping my clit and I moan. I wrap my arms around his neck and bring his lips to mine as I begin to rock beneath him, rubbing my wet sex against his cock. "God, I can feel how wet you are." I point and flex my feet, desperate to rub my clit against his dick at the right angle that would have me shattering around him. He bites my bottom lip before sucking it into his mouth and licking the sting of his teeth away.

"Lose your underwear. *Please*," I moan.

"Lose your bra. *Now.*"

I sit up slightly, unhooking my bra and tossing it off my bed, leaving me completely naked beneath him. His hands are on my breasts instantly, rolling and stimulating my nipples before he places kisses on both of them. "There's so much I want to do to your body. Fuck." He sits back on his heels and scans my body from my eyes to my sex, before meeting my gaze again. *"Voglio scoparti."*

Translation? I want to fuck you.

"Sì, per favore," I tell him. *Yes, please.*

"But I need a taste first. Indulge me, Princess." I don't have a chance to respond before his hands are on my thighs, opening me up for him and his mouth is on my pussy. *Oh, dear God.* His thumbs rub my inner thighs so erotically it almost feels like it's on my sex. "Let me hear you." He takes his time, exploring my folds and fucking me with his tongue, completely avoiding my clitoris. His tongue is warm and firm, stroking my sex in ways no one ever has. *I want to pin this man down and ride his face for the rest of my life.* "Scream for me, baby."

"Oh God, Aidan, right there," I whimper as I grab ahold of his silky, mahogany hair and tug gently.

He pulls back and slaps my sex gently with his hand and I yelp but it comes out more like a moan. I feel my clit pulse and my entire pussy clenches with desire and anticipation. "I want to submerge my face in your cunt and live there," he growls. "Do you have any idea how good you taste?" He rubs two fingers through my sex and before I can think they're in front of my mouth. "Open."

I'll admit I was curious about how I tasted, but no one had ever urged me to try, and it felt odd to taste it after I masturbated. I wrap my lips around his fingers, sucking them like I would his cock and he groans. "Jesus, Skyler."

"Please, can you get a condom?" I was starting to feel frantic. A frenzy moving through my body as it craved the orgasm that I was seconds away from when he was tonguing my pussy.

He stands up and pushes his underwear down his legs

revealing a powerful erection that would make me weak in the knees if I were standing. I sit up on my elbows and follow his cock with my eyes as he opens the box. "Wow," I whisper and a chuckle leaves his lips as he joins me back on the bed.

"I'm glad you like what you see."

"Who *wouldn't* like that?" For a moment I could swear I saw a fleeting look I can't place, but it's gone as soon as it comes making me wonder if I imagined it, or if the candle-light glow is playing tricks on me. "I haven't…I mean you'll be the biggest and…"

He almost growls at me as he pushes me down and forces my legs apart. "I don't want to hear about anyone that's touched this pussy before me. Understand?"

Oh my God.

"Let's get a few things clear, Skyler," he whispers against my lips. "I don't share. *Ever.* So, if you let me inside you…You are mine."

I gulp. "Yes. Yours."

His hand moves up my body and wraps around my throat slightly. "Do you trust me?" I don't say anything for a second and he lets his hand go. "I would never hurt you." He gives me a shy smile. "I want to show you how good it can feel. You don't know your body. But I'm going to teach you what it can do in the right hands." He leans down and brushes his lips over mine.

"By choking me?" He smiles again and for the first time in a while, I feel the rush of adventure. "I'm game."

I watch as he slides back on his heels and opens the condom, then slides it onto the hard appendage that is all but purple and leaking cum already. "I will make you come with my mouth later. But right now, I can't wait another second without being inside of you."

He holds his cock in his right hand, while his left, wraps around my throat again. He taps my clit with his cock and I jolt. He squeezes my throat in perfect synchronization and I'm already seeing stars when he pushes inside of me forcefully.

"FUCK!" we both cry out in unison.

"You are so fucking tight, Skyler, fuck!"

"You are s—so b—big," I groan as he pulls out and pushes in again, almost knocking the wind out of me that wasn't being cut off by his hand in the process.

"You're squeezing me so fucking tight. Milk my cock, princess." He squeezes my throat, with every thrust he does so a bit tighter. I let my eyes flutter closed when I feel his lips ghost across mine. *"Sei perfetta,"* I hear him whisper, but he sounds far away. My senses are numb, the only one heightened is the sense of feeling and right now every single nerve in my body is pulled and stretched taut, desperate for the release that is only seconds away.

Sei perfetta. You are perfect. The tears form in my eyes and when I open them, he's staring down at me, his face a mix of intense passion and determination. His other hand, not wrapped around my throat, wipes the tear that leaked out of my eyes, down the side of my face and into my hair. *He was right. I would cry.*

"Skyler, I need you to come for me. Please." I grab his hand that's wrapped around my throat and I squeeze urging him to do it harder and he does as his thrusts get more aggressive.

The feeling in the base of my spine intensifies and I feel like I'm being split open. "Aidan... I'm going to..."

"That's a good girl, tell me what you're feeling," he whispers.

"Feels s—so good," I manage to get out between breaths that are slowly leaving my body. Spots appear in my peripheral vision, and I close my eyes focusing on the tingles congregating in my sex and beginning to move through my body on a mission. With one final thrust, my eyes pop open and the spark ignites a fire within. "Oh my—" I start and he lets go of my throat. I gasp for air, as the force of my orgasm has knocked it out of me. "Oh my God. Oh my God. Oh my God!" I moan as I drag my nails down his back. He lets out a guttural moan, from deep in his throat and comes with a roar.

"SKYLER. FUCK." I don't know how long his orgasm lasts as I'm still feeling the effects of mine, but when my eyes flutter open again, his lips are leaving languid kisses on my neck and trailing down my chest every few seconds.

"Sei incredibile," he mumbles against my skin just before he pulls out of me.

"You're pretty incredible too." I suddenly feel cold with the loss of his body heat, and I wonder if he's going to leave when I see him roll the condom up and tie it off before tossing it in my trashcan. I happen to catch a glance at his dick, and while it's softened significantly it's still magnificent. I reach for him when he climbs on the bed and I run my hand over it.

"Your dick is amazing."

He all but tackles me and presses his lips to mine, once I'm secured underneath him. "It certainly loves your pussy." I wrap my arms around his neck and he kisses my arm. He leans back slightly and moves my arm so he can read my tattoo. He squints slightly. "It's a little dark in here, what does it say?"

"Life goes on, in Italian."

"La Vita va Avanti."

I groan and wrap my legs around him, pressing his dick into my sex. "Don't speak Italian to me unless you're planning to fuck me again."

"Oh, I'm definitely planning to fuck you again. Many more times. This time with my mouth." He grins before he descends down my body.

Lips rubbing against my neck and a sensation below rouses me from sleep. I wonder how long it's been since the last time Aidan woke me up. We barely slept all night, having woken up multiple times to fuck or fool around. The last time, was around 6 AM. The sun peeked through my blinds just as I rested my pussy onto his wanting mouth and wrapped my lips around his cock.

I moan and turn in his arms, bummed that this isn't going to result in round-whatever when I notice he's fully dressed in last night's clothes. "Morning, beautiful."

I press the back of my hand to my mouth to stifle a yawn. "You're leaving? What time is it?"

"As much as I want to stay in this bed with your warm body that was rubbing up against me this morning, I gotta go. I have to take Chace to the airport in a few hours." He points at my coffee table. "I made some coffee."

Don't tell him you love him, Sky.

"Thank you. For…the coffee and, you know, the great sex."

He laughs and pulls out his phone. "Well, I would like to see you again…for more great sex." He hands me his phone. "Can I have your number?"

I take his phone and add my number while he reaches for mine to add his. "You know if you find yourself bored later, you could always…come back?" I get out of bed and grab my robe off the back of the door, but not before hearing him groan as his eyes trail my naked body.

I look back at him and his eyes are still trained on my breasts even though I've now covered up. He gets off the bed and makes his way towards me. "As much as I would love that, I actually have to get ready for tomorrow."

"Tomorrow?"

"First day." He smiles as I follow him towards the door.

"You know, I don't think I even know what you do." I giggle and he presses a kiss to my lips.

"No, I don't think we got to that. I took a teaching job at CGU."

"Oh?!" There's a tremor in my voice and I hear a slight squeak that I hope he misses. "What uh… what class or field…" I trip over my words, my body in full on panic mode that I might run into this man on campus after I'd lied about essentially everything.

"Jesus. One sec. What Chace?" he growls. "Yes, I'm coming. Hold your horses." He hangs up and looks down at me.

"Oh…I can take you home? I have my car."

"No, Chace drove my car. He's downstairs, but thank you. Listen, I can bore you with all the details about work tomorrow over dinner?" He cups my cheeks with both hands and leans in to kiss me softly. "I had fun."

"Me too." I bite my lip as I think about how Aidan is going to blow a gasket when he finds out I'm a student at CGU.

Maybe I don't have to tell him? I mean it's a big school. He may never even know. There's thirty thousand of us. What are the chances we'll run into each other?

Even as I think the thoughts, I don't believe them.

Life might go on…

But she could be a real bitch.

Aidan

I jog down the stairs of Skyler's building, the nerves of the night and this morning still running haywire. It took everything out of me not to tell Chace just to fucking Uber to the airport so I could stay holed up in Skyler's bed with her all day, her sexy body pressed against—I huff in annoyance at the fact that I have to take this asshole to the airport.

Well, he is the reason you met Skyler.

Chace is parked out front, with every window down, blasting music out of my Wrangler. I approach the car and he's grinning from ear to ear. "Can you turn that shit down? It's early. And it's Sunday."

He turns the music down with a dramatic eye roll. "Awww, is Aidy boy cranky that he had to pull himself out of the hot Italian?"

"What did I tell you about calling her that?" I growl as I settle into the passenger seat. Before I was annoyed, but now I'm pissed. *Skyler isn't the hot Italian. Well, she is hot, but...* He chuckles before he pulls his sunglasses from his face. "Bro, tell me you got laid."

"Did you?" I ask. "Did you defile the bed in my guestroom?"

"Guestroom?" he snorts.

My head snaps to look at him. "If you fucked that girl in my bed, I'll kill you."

"Relax, your sheets are in the wash." He waves me off.

"Are you fucking kidding me, Chace?"

"What?"

"You're such a fucking dick."

"Oh chill the fuck out." He pulls away from her building and starts driving back to my apartment, which if I'm totally honest, I have no idea where it is. "So, did you smash or nah?"

I know if I don't give him something he'll literally be like a dog with a bone, and normally I wouldn't mind indulging him, but Skyler feels…different. "We had sex," I tell him as I rub a hand over my face. The fatigue of getting no sleep last night is catching up with me. *Worth it though.* "A lot of sex." Skyler is undoubtedly the hottest girl I've ever fucked, and I swear her pussy felt like a vice was wrapped around my dick when I was inside of her. She gave head like she was made to do it, and her pussy tasted like sin and sex. I shift in my seat thinking about the way she rode my face this morning, her cum dribbling down my chin and sinking into my skin. *Fuck, I still smell her on me.*

"Finally! God, I knew all it would take is one night out with yours truly. James can go fuck himself." He turns down a familiar street and I take note of how fast we got here from Skyler's apartment. "So, you going to see her again?"

I can't stop the smile from spreading across my face. "Tomorrow."

"Word? A date?" He pulls into my garage and into my parking spot.

"We're having dinner."

"And by dinner you mean..." He makes the gesture for a blow job and I'm out of the car instantly. "Oh, come on, when did you get to be so uptight? Before the ice queen removed your dick from your body, you would have appreciated that. I thought when you guys broke up she gave you your balls back?" He follows me into my building.

"Because I'm not twenty fucking seven anymore. Excuse me for having just a bit of respect for women."

"Oh God. Here we go." He groans as we enter my apartment.

"What?"

"You're going to get all weird and scare this girl off. I can already tell."

"No, I'm not."

"C'mon it's just us. Lay off. I'm not asking what her cunt tasted like in fucking front of her. Get that stick out of your ass before I knock it out. I made a few jokes about fucking her and you're ready to have a fit. I know it's been a while since you've been in the game, but just...keep it chill. You don't have to be so intense."

"I am chill."

"And she's your rebound! I know how you think. Don't pin all your hopes and dreams on this young girl, Aidan. You'll just get hurt. She's here to have fun, not take the Reed name."

"I'm not trying to marry her, Jesus Chace. I've done the casual sex thing."

"Alright. Just...be careful, bro. Don't go too hard, too fast." He pauses. "Well...you know what I mean." He smirks and raises his eyebrows up and down at his innuendo.

I heed Chace's warnings. My natural response to what happened last night is to text Skyler. Ask her how her day is going and maybe what color her panties are. I don't and now it's the next day. I would never say this to Chace, but I haven't stopped thinking about her since I left her apartment yesterday morning and it irritates me more than I care to admit that I didn't talk to her again last night. *Don't come on too strong. Be aloof,* Chace told me.

Did that shit really work? Or did she just think I was ghosting her? But if I texted her, then I was too intense? God, the line was so blurry, I didn't know which side I was standing on. I stare at the ceiling, waiting for my alarm to go off and my dick to go down, making me wonder if I should just go ahead and jack off, when I hear the sounds of a text message notification. I turn my head to my phone wondering who the hell is texting me at 7 AM. My eyes snap open further when I see the message.

Skyler: Have a good first day! No dad jokes, and you'll be fine.

I am the furthest thing from a morning person, and the fact that she got me to crack a smile before the sun had fully risen has to be some kind of miracle.

Aidan: I do not make dad jokes! I don't remember you doing a whole lot of laughing Saturday night.
Skyler: True. But you seem like the kind that might crack one when you're nervous hehe
Aidan: I am not nervous. I've done this before, I'll have you know.
Skyler: In Boston?
Aidan: Mmmhmm

> Skyler: What made you come here?
> Aidan: I haven't had coffee yet. Too early for that conversation. Why are you up so early anyway?
> Skyler: Class at 8

What grad student chooses a class at 8 AM? When I was in grad school, I planned it so I only had class three days a week and my days didn't start until eleven. *Rookie mistake.*

> Aidan: Woof. Sounds like the worst idea ever. You never did tell me what you were studying anyway?
> Skyler: Criminal Justice
> Aidan: No shit? That's what I'm teaching at CGU. I knew I liked you.

Well, at least I knew we had things in common besides our obsession with each other's genitals. I'd studied Criminal Justice in undergrad, Social Justice in grad school, and got my doctorate in Criminal Justice. Once I realized that I had no interest in going to law school, I'd spent some time working at a non-profit in Boston. *Something Corinne hated.* There was little to no money in it, and she had wanted a very expensive ring. Harvard had wanted my knowledge. I'd been published in over a dozen textbooks and co-wrote a book with my mentor two years before, so I had the skills, but I didn't exactly have the passion to teach a bunch of eighteen year olds who didn't give a fuck about much other than getting the A and just regurgitating the words I'd spoken. Nevertheless, I pressed on, and I actually didn't hate it as much as I thought I would.

I look at my phone and notice she hasn't responded. Chace would probably be rolling his eyes at me right now.

> Aidan: Have a good day. I'll text you later about dinner.

Skyler

"Fuck." I toss my phone on my bed as I scramble to finish getting ready for class. I'd put off messaging him all day yesterday, knowing I'd needed to figure out just what he was teaching, but I was too much of a chicken to do it. I pull on my gray leather jacket over a white t-shirt and slide my sunglasses into my hair. I slip my feet into flats and do a spin in the mirror, taking in my outfit. I look down at my bare legs, extending from a black mini-skirt, and I am pleased that I still have a good tan.

There's a knock at my door and I call towards it. "It's open, Peyton!" I'd offered to drive her to campus today because one, I didn't know exactly where to go or where to park, and two, Peyton had actually grown on me.

"I brought coffee!" *Oh, and she offered to bring coffee.* "Even though I believe it was you, *Bella,* that was supposed to bring *me* coffee for getting you some hot sex with Boston Hottie!" She shoots me a look as she hands me a cup of the steaming liquid that I pray will make me feel better.

I ignore her comment, because right now despite the hot sex I had, I could strangle her for getting me into my current predicament. "He's a fucking Criminal Justice professor. I'm going to have him as a professor, I just know it!" I shriek as soon as she enters my bedroom.

"Well, isn't this just a comedy of errors?" Peyton shakes her head and plops down on my bed, pressing the paper cup to her lips as she stifles a giggle.

"Peyton, this isn't funny. He is going to fucking lose it. Why did I listen to you about changing my age?! He wouldn't have paid me a second look if he knew I was nineteen."

"What makes you think that? You're hot, Sky. Like really hot. AND guys like younger girls. The closer you are to jailbait the better." She points at me.

I scrunch my nose and shake my head. "Aidan isn't like that."

"Oh, and you know that because of all the time he spent inside of you? You're right, Sky, he fucked a girl he just met on the first night, on his first weekend in a new city, from an app he joined for the sole purpose of casual sex..." She gives me a thumbs-up. "He really gives a fuck that you lied about your age."

"He's going to care when I show up in his class!"

"Then you transfer out." She rolls her eyes and blows her hair from her eyes. "You're being really dramatic, and I haven't finished this cup yet."

"I'm going to shit my pants if I have him as a teacher."

"Don't you have like a schedule or something?" I hear the sarcasm dripping from her voice. "Why don't you just check?"

"Brilliant! But I don't know his last name." I grab my schedule from my bag.

"His first name should still be on there." I sit on my bed scanning my schedule and I breathe a sigh of relief when I don't see *Aidan* listed anywhere on my schedule. "See you're panicking for nothing. So, he's teaching in your major but it doesn't mean you'll have him."

"You're right, and I'll tell him tonight at dinner. And if he hates me and never wants to see me again, at least I can rest assured that I won't have to face him every day."

"Exactly. Now, come on, the parking lot is a traffic jam in the mornings."

I'd gotten through two classes already, my heart pounding out of my chest through the first ten minutes of each just waiting for Aidan to manifest. By noon, I was starting to calm down, knowing that, one, I'd be getting lunch with Peyton soon, and two, I might make it through the day without any run-ins. I've even opted for a seat in the second row of the sixty person lecture. In the other two classes, I'd sat in the back, something I hated, but I was so worried he'd show up, I knew I needed an escape method, or at least to be able to hide behind someone tall. But I prefer to sit in the front. I'm not thrilled about being back in school, but I'll admit I was a teacher's pet. A girl sits next to me, dropping her bag on the floor and begins to fluff her red wavy hair in a compact mirror. "So, what do you think he'll look like?"

I look around wondering who she's talking to. "I beg your pardon?"

"The new professor. I hear he's gorgeous."

"Wh—what?"

"There's a change in the syllabus, didn't you get the email last week?" She doesn't look at me, as she has now taken out a tube of lipstick and has begun reapplying.

"Umm... no? I mean...I don't think so? I was having an

issue with my emails until this morning." My heart begins to race in my chest. *I was almost home free. Fuck. Fuck. Fuck.*

"Ah, well the initial professor had a conflict in the schedule or his wife had a baby or something. Anyway, we have a new professor."

My heart races at her words. "And…"

"And word on the street is he's gorgeous. Like, total babe."

"Do…do you know his name?"

"Ummm, I'm blanking." She pulls her phone out. "I'm Lily."

"Sk—Skyler," I stutter, my body slowly shutting down as it braces for impact. *Oh my God. Oh my God.* I turn around in the class and notice that the seats are all starting to fill up. *Maybe I should just leave before he gets here.* I start to stand when the door opens and the object of my fantasies for the past day and a half comes strutting into the room looking even better than he did on Saturday. I immediately plant myself back in my seat just as I hear a "hot as fuck" fall from Lily's lips.

I put a hand over my eyes and turn away from him as much as I can. *You gonna hide for fifty minutes, Sky?*

The class is set up like an atrium, with each row of seats slightly higher than the one in front of it, and I'm grateful to be more off to the side so I'm not in his direct line of sight.

"Good afternoon everyone, I'm Doctor Aidan Reed and this is Social Justice 101. I realize that there's a slight difference in the syllabus, but I do believe that everyone should have received the email that Professor Billings would not be your teacher this semester. If that serves to be a problem for anyone, please come talk to me. I promise, I'm a really nice guy. And I'll probably let you turn your final in a day late." He chuckles and everyone in the class cheers. *Except me.* I'm sweating in my seat, actual beads of sweat form on my forehead, and I still haven't looked at him. Even now, I can't even enjoy the fact that the best sex of my life is within twenty feet of me.

"I don't really have many rules. Be on time. Eating is fine. Computers are fine. Just be respectful of the people around you. Wherever you've chosen to sit is your seat for the semester so I hope you're comfortable. I'm passing around a seating chart that I'll pass around at the start of every class. Now, frankly, I don't care if you come to class or not, but if you choose to come, there's something in it for you. If you attend every class you can get up to five extra credit points at the end of the semester. Those points fluctuate if you miss a class."

Great. No skipping.

"God, he's hot, right?" Lily whispers and I don't respond. *God girl, hush! Don't draw his attention over here.* "I mean I've never had a hot teacher…do you think, he'll offer office hours?" *Back off bitch,* my subconscious perks up.

Not fucking now! Aren't I in enough trouble?

I still haven't looked at her or even towards Aidan and my eyes are now screwed shut, willing the fifty minutes by faster.

"Do you have a question, miss?" *Fuck. Don't look. Do not look.*

"Oh. Umm no. Sorry," I hear Lily squeak out. *You just couldn't shut the fuck up.*

"How about you, miss, trying to pretend she doesn't know I'm talking to her." He chuckles and the entire class snickers. My face flushes bright red as I prepare to meet my fate. I turn slightly, and when my eyes meet his, I have a flash of Saturday night. Writhing underneath him, screaming his name into the dark room. His mouth on me, his cock inside of me, his lips on mine. He must be having the same thoughts because his eyes widen and his mouth drops open though he recovers rather quickly, averting his gaze from mine. "Right, well, if no one has any questions, then we can proceed."

For the next fifty minutes, time actually stands still. The second the minute ticks to twelve fifty I want nothing more than to haul ass out of there, but I know I need to face Aidan. *Without prying eyes.* I stay seated and wait as my classmates file out. I watch as Lily and a few other girls wait in line to talk to him. I cross my arms, watching as they shamelessly flirt with him while I seethe. *If I can't have him, you certainly can't. Stop embarrassing yourself.*

After ten minutes of watching this fucking charade, and ignoring two of Peyton's phone calls and texts wondering if I had gotten lost on the way to the quad for lunch, I get up, pull my sunglasses over my eyes and proceed to strut past *Doctor Reed* and his groupies.

Am I fucking jealous? Do I really crave his attention that bad? When I was hoping to avoid it for most of the morning?

I've barely taken two steps out of the classroom, a sigh of relief leaving my lips, when I feel a hand wrap around my elbow and I'm being pulled *hard* through the halls. "Ai—Doctor Reed…" I say as I struggle, *yet again,* to keep up with his strides. He doesn't say anything for the entire walk, down one hall and then down another. I watch as he puts his key in a door and then I'm being pushed inside and he slams it behind us. I realize as he flicks the lights on that we're in his office and I suddenly feel claustrophobic, enclosed in this small space with this man and our raging hormones.

Well, maybe just mine.

He might have something else raging.

"WHAT THE FUCK, SKYLER!?" he booms and I shake slightly at his tone.

I run through a bunch of scenarios in my head, trying to figure out what the best course of action is before I turn around and face him, pulling my sunglasses from my face and sliding them into my bag.

Cry.
Seduce him.
Yell.
Blame him.
Play dumb.
All of the above?

I turn around and wince slightly. "Okay, you're pissed. Umm…but, well, see…" I don't say anything for a moment and when I meet his gaze, I can see the fury softening.

"Tell me you're at least eighteen." I can sense the panic in his voice and I'm happy I can at least ease those fears.

"Yes!" I say quickly. "I'm nineteen. I took a year off after high school, I told you."

"Oh. You told me? You told me a lot of things. Glad to know you can tell the truth about *some* things." He shakes his head. "You said you were a grad student. And TWENTY-TWO. How the fuck did you even get into that bar?"

I cock my head to the side as if to say, *what do you think?*

"God, I fucked a girl that still has to use a fake ID. Christ, Skyler, I'm thirty fucking two. And your TEACHER."

"Well, you see…we didn't know that exactly at the time." I trail off. *Right because that's the point.* I give him my most innocent smile.

"Don't be fucking cute. Now is really not the fucking time." He growls as he slams his hand on his desk.

"I'm sorry!"

"For being a liar or what?" he snaps and I have to admit his words sting, but I have nothing to say for myself. I mean, he's right, I lied.

"Aidan…"

"Doctor Reed. I'm your teacher, Skyler."

"Girls lie about their age all the time and I just…I didn't know…" I trail off. I'm grasping at straws and I actually don't have an argument. "I really am sorry. But it's no harm, I'll just transfer out of your class."

"All of the other social justice classes are full this semester." He sits at his desk and rubs a hand through his hair. "It's good that I learned this now, anyway. Even if you weren't my student, I couldn't be with someone who just lied straight to my face."

"I didn't…we didn't really talk about what we were doing here…"

"You led me to believe you were a twenty-two year old grad student, Skyler. Don't bullshit me. You lied by omission. Actually, fuck omission. You flat out lied. And I don't date liars. So, you're dismissed."

His words eviscerate me. I had never been called a liar before and it crushes me, even if it is the truth. "Excuse me?"

"You heard me. You need to go."

"You can't talk to me like that. I get it, you're pissed, but you're being a dick."

"Yeah, and if you don't want me to fail you, I suggest you go." He rubs his hand over his face and points toward the door behind me.

"If you think I won't go way the fuck over your head, you have another thing coming. I'm the biggest legacy of this fucking school. The Chancellor is my Godfather for crying out loud."

He snorts. "Of course he is, princess."

I flex my fists, trying my hardest not to cry, or hit him, or both. Tears lodge in the back of my throat as I take a deep breath and try to calm myself. "Listen, I'm sorry that we're in this mess, but being an asshole to me isn't helping. So, how about you actually come up with something that's actually *helpful* instead of insulting me."

"I already advised you to *go*."

He's not looking at me, his eyes are focused on his computer as he pulls at his hair. "Fine. Don't expect me in class on Wednesday. You can take those five points and shove them up your ass," I snap.

I turn around and open the door when a hand darts out in my periphery, slamming it closed. I hear his heavy breathing right behind me and his hand still rests on the door before I watch it ball into a fist. "Skyler," he whispers and his voice is pained, not angry like he's been for this entire conversation.

I swallow, feeling the tension crackle between us as I turn around and stare up into his blue eyes that are showing a wide range of emotions. For a moment, it's as if time stops. We're only staring at each other, our eyes having a silent conversation that I'm not sure I even understood. But then my hands are on his belt and his hands are in my hair, his lips on mine, kissing, biting, sucking, licking. And just like that, a flood of different emotions come rushing back. His hands cup my cheeks as his tongue invades my mouth and I'm reminded how good he tastes. He pulls away only to find the space behind my ear that he'd discovered makes me weak. My knees buckle, but he holds me up before he lifts me into his arms pressing me hard against the door. Large hands grope my breasts and a guttural moan leaves my lips.

Fuck, you drive me crazy," he whispers in my ear as I feel

his hands drop to my butt and he drives his cock against me. "Take it out, Skyler," he growls. "Take it out so I can fuck you." I do as he says, sending his slacks down his legs and pulling his cock out of his briefs.

God, it's more perfect than I remembered! "Aidan," I whimper.

"Hold on, baby."

I wrap my legs around his waist and my arms around his neck, clinging to him as he pulls my underwear from under my skirt with one loud *rip*.

I watch as they fall to the floor and within a second he's inside of me. "FUCK." He starts to fuck me relentlessly, harder and faster than he did on Saturday.

"Oh my God!" I cry, my clit already tingling as I prepare for my release when he freezes. My eyes fly open and I meet his gaze.

"Condom," he says through gritted teeth and I can feel his cock pulsing inside of me.

"Pill," I answer.

"You're on it?" he asks and I nod. "What the fuck for?" he barks, and I shoot him a look that says *who the fuck do you think you are?*

"I mean…" He looks around the room before turning back to me. His eyes are squeezed shut almost painfully "Just the thought of you fucking someone else pisses me off."

"I'm not," I whisper.

"But I can't fuck you either."

"You surely picked a fine time to come to that realization." I raise an eyebrow at him before darting my gaze down to where we're connected.

A smile plays on his lips. "I'm going to finish us off, but then that's it…I can't…we can't be reckless, Skyler."

"Fine." *But I was anything but fine.* He begins to push in and out of me harder, going further than anyone has ever gone. At this angle he's in, I feel deliciously full every time he buries himself to the hilt.

"Fucking fuck. This sucks," he laments in a gruff voice.

I nod in response, my lips dragging along his neck. He wraps his arms around me, essentially using me to jack himself off as he moves *me* up and down on his dick. *Damn this man is strong.*

"I'm going to come, baby. I don't want to come inside of you."

"Do you want to come in my mouth?" I purr in his ear and he grabs my head by my hair and yanks me back to look at me.

His eyes stare at me, hard, before he lets himself fall out of me and I scramble to my knees. His cock is down my throat before I can think and I wrap my hands around his ass and squeeze. *I'm going to miss this ass. And this cock. God, he truly is a perfect specimen.*

"Fuck, Skyler." He wraps his hands in my hair as he meets my face with every suck. Drool pools in the corners of my mouth. His cock tastes like my pussy and for some reason it turns me on even more. "Your mouth is insane," he whispers. I catch a peek upwards and I see his head is thrown back as he thrusts into my wanting mouth. I reach between his legs and find his balls, fondling them in my hands and he erupts instantly down my throat. "Fuuuuuck!" he groans as streams of cum shoot out of his dick and into my mouth. I swallow everything he has to offer before he lets his cock slide from his lips. Realization of what we just did hits me like a ton of bricks, and I can't even look up and see the look of disgust that he probably has all over his face now that he's come. "Hey," he says as he lifts my chin up to meet his gaze. He reaches down and hauls me to my feet. "Why the face?"

I told myself I wasn't going to cry, but in this moment, I feel like nothing more than a space for him to deposit his cum. The word *cumdumpster* flashes through my mind and I hate that I feel so cheap. "You're so angry with me," I whisper and I feel the tears forming in my eyes. "You just spent the past ten minutes screaming at me and making me feel like shit and then… you fucked me, and now you're going to hate me again, and I feel…used, to be honest."

"Skyler, look at me," he orders me, and when I do I notice his blue eyes are significantly softer. "I'm sorry for how I spoke to you. That was just…my shit. It wasn't about you."

"You sure about that?" I ask.

He sighs and moves to the small couch in the room and sits down, offering me a seat next to him. I do, creating a bit of space between us, but still feeling close enough that I know he could probably smell the mix of our arousals on my sex. "My ex lied about…a lot of things. I guess it still messes with my head a little…when someone lies to me."

I nod, knowing exactly how he feels after my own history with a liar. "Aidan, I'm sorry."

"Me too, Skyler."

"So, this…is it?" I ask.

"Afraid so, princess." I nod once before I stand up and I prepare to leave, grabbing my destroyed underwear and stuffing them in my bag. "Wait," he whispers.

I turn towards him and he presses his lips to mine. The kiss is slow and passionate, a contrast to the animalistic, aggressive kiss from earlier that left my lips bruised and swollen. His tongue moves against mine in perfect rhythm when I feel his hand between my legs. I pull back and look at him.

"What are you doing?"

"You didn't come." He lifts my skirt slightly and parts my

legs further. "I need to make you come one last time." He rests his forehead against mine as he glides his fingers through my sex, rubbing my clit in between strokes. *"Mi mancherai, Bella."* *I'll miss you, Bella.*

"I'll miss you too," I whisper.

I find myself trying to prolong the orgasm, knowing that once it comes, it's the end. Aidan and I are over.

That thought hits me harder than the orgasm.

Skyler

"**A**BOUT TIME YOU SHOWED UP." PEYTON QUIPS AS I SET my bag down across from her. "You're lucky I don't have problems eating by myself. A more insecure girl would have your head, Skyler Mitchell." I found her on the quad, parked on a picnic bench taking selfies in between bites of her kale salad. She takes in my expression and blanches. "Oh shit. Run into Aidan?"

"Oh yeah." I prop my elbows up on the table and put my head in my hands. "I am so fucked." I remember that I'm naked under my skirt. *Literally.*

"What happened?"

"I'm in his class."

Peyton goes through a series of emotions that I can read all over her face, from shock to worry to dread as she rubs her nose ring. "I thought…you said you didn't see his name?"

"There was a last minute change of Professor. He walked in. He saw me. Froze. I turned fifty shades of red but he played it off well. After class, he dragged me to his office, proceeded to hand my ass to me for ten minutes and then we fucked without a condom and he came in my mouth."

Peyton chokes on her salad and begins coughing before downing a large gulp of water. "You guys fucked?"

"Yeah." My stomach turns and for a second I wonder if I should eat something, but I have a feeling it'll come right back up.

"Without a condom?"

"It was…impulsive."

"Clearly," she snorts.

"He says that was the end."

"Well, maybe just 'till the end of the semester?"

"He's angry at me for lying to him. I think this is the end period."

She rolls her eyes and scoffs. "The holier than thou approach, I see." I lay my hands flat on the table and rest my forehead against them. "Sky, I'm sorry."

I'm exhausted. It's only noon and I feel like I could crawl into bed and sleep for a week. I'm humiliated and hurt and pissed at myself, and yet I can't control the throbbing between my legs that he'd caused when he rubbed me to an orgasm not ten minutes ago. I'm very aware that I don't have underwear on, and every time the wind blows I feel the breeze tickle my wet sex and I have to stifle a moan.

"Go figure, the best sex of my life and I only get it twice."

"There will be other guys. We'll go out tonight! First week of the semester, there's always tons of parties."

I pick my head up and shake it back and forth. "Peyton, I'm really not in the mood."

She purses her lips before nodding once and sliding her sunglasses over her eyes. "Fine." She points her fork at me. "You have one day to be sad. Tomorrow, we party. Alright? Come on Sky, like you say, *life goes on.*"

It was the first time I'd ever hated hearing those words.

I spent the evening in bed after doing a bit of studying from the day's classes. *Including a certain Doctor Reed's.* I'd eventually given up and climbed into bed with *Sex and the City* and a pint of mint chocolate chip ice cream. It isn't until halfway through Samantha getting nailed by some hot random guy that I realize, I'm fucking horny. My mind drifts back to his arms wrapped around me, his cock inside of me. *His bare cock.* I had never felt anything so intimate. Nothing between us. No barriers. I let out a breath as I think about how reckless we were. How much I wanted to be reckless again. *And again. And again.*

My fingers itch to text him. That familiar tingle that comes when you're really into a guy and you feel flutters in your stomach at the idea of talking to him.

He's not going to answer, Skyler. He's probably already blocked you.

I'm his student though, what if I have a question about the class?

Then you email him like students are advised, my subconscious sneers.

Just as my hands find my phone I remember Stella's words of wisdom. "If you're thinking about sending a risky text to someone you probably shouldn't, masturbate first. If you cum and you still want to, go for it. But a horny mind is a dangerous thing. Rub one out before you text." I can hear her words clear as day as she adjusts those glasses that has every guy in a ten mile radius referring to her as a sexy librarian. "This does not apply if you're drunk. If that's the case…delete the text after you send so that tomorrow, 'sober you' isn't privy to the damage."

I drop my phone like it's on fire and my hand flies to the space between my legs, sliding my hand under the elastic of my shorts. "Fuck. Aidan. WHY?!" I whine as I rub my finger over my clit and further down to the space inside. "I can't even fucking finger myself the way he does it." I throw my covers off me, letting the cool air hit my legs as I try to picture Aidan's mouth between my legs. I open one eye praying that he appears before me.

"Che cosa desideri, Bella?" I can almost hear his words. *What is my desire? You're my desire, Aidan. Fuck, I want you so god damn much.*

"Tell me how much." My clit pulses as I picture him in his office, so close I can taste his breath, hear his heart beating in his chest. His voice is almost pained as he looks me over, the regret all over his perfect features as realization washes all over his face. *"I can't stop thinking about you, Skyler."*

"Just one more time, please?"

He crosses the length of his office until he's standing before me. *"One more time isn't enough."*

"I know." I'm soaking wet at this point, my fingers gliding easily over the sensitive nerves every few seconds. He undoes his pants, letting them fall and I take a moment to drool over the perfection of his cock. *"Your dick is a masterpiece,"* I murmur, and quick as lightning he's on me, his cock inside of me and his hand wrapped around my throat as he fucks me hard against his office door.

"You'll be my undoing, Skyler."

"Ditto." I manage as he closes his hand harder around my windpipe.

His thrusts get more aggressive and my fingers work overtime to get me to the orgasm that is just a beat away. "Fuck. AIDAN!" I scream as the tingles turn into an explosion that rips through my body. My eyes fly open at the peak of my orgasm and I fly over the edge as my body comes down from the high. I slide my hand from between my legs and stare at my fingers. They're coated with my cum and I remember the heady feeling of sucking myself off of him.

"Go ahead baby, taste yourself. You know you want to."

Before I can think that these are *not* his fingers, they're in my mouth.

I look at my phone again. *Don't do it, Skyler. You know nothing good will come from it.*

I turn over on my side with a huff, and somehow with the feeling still tingling between my legs and the flavors of my orgasm lingering in my mouth, sleep finds me.

I toss and turn for the majority of the night, leaving me with some ridiculous bags under my eyes that I'm doing my best to cover up with dark sunglasses. I'm sitting in the courtyard near the Criminal Justice building trying to distract myself from how tired I am and how much hornier I am when a shadow is cast over my textbook. I look up, unsure of what to expect when my eyes widen slightly.

"Ai—Doctor Reed." I clear my throat, trying my best not to sound like the needy girl that spent the night switching between fantasizing about him and pissed off that I *couldn't* stop fantasizing about him. Sunglasses hide his eyes as well, and I briefly wonder if his bags match mine. His hair is a little more unkempt than it was yesterday, and he's not wearing a tie. Just a white button up tucked into navy slacks. His shirt is rolled up to his elbows revealing muscular arms. *Ones I would now spend the rest of the day picturing wrapped around me as he mercilessly fucked me.*

"Skyler." He sits next to me but he doesn't say anything further. I take a peek at him as best as I can from the corner of my eye and notice his jaw tightens slightly and he's fidgeting with his hands. *What is happening?*

"I can't stop thinking about you." My mind immediately goes to my fantasy last night and for a brief moment my mind makes me believe that I hadn't imagined that. That it actually happened.

I really am losing it. It's official, dickmatization can make you actually insane.

"I spent the entire night..." he trails off, and I wonder if he's talking more to himself because he stops and turns towards me. "I know I should probably stay away from you." I go to reply when he continues. "But...you are..." He lets out a breath before he stands, and I realize I haven't said anything during this whole interaction. "You're nineteen..." He looks away from me before running a hand through his hair. "If I were nineteen, I'd spend more time studying your God damn anatomy than anything." He shakes his head and takes a step back like he's remembered himself. "But I'm not. Sorry I bothered you," he mumbles before he turns to leave.

"Aidan," I call after him.

He doesn't turn around but he stops walking. "No Skyler." His shoulders sag and I hear that pain in his voice from last night.

"But..."

"No," he says before he turns slightly to look back at me. "You look beautiful." And then he's gone, leaving me with my very confused thoughts and the wish that I had texted him last night so we could have done what we were clearly both doing, *together.*

The very weird interaction I had with Aidan earlier leaves me on edge for much of the day. I'm so out of sorts that, without even realizing it, I end up in front of his office door after my last class of the day.

I raise my hand to knock when I hear, "Excuse me, but there's a line." The bitchy tone is evident and when I turn my head, there are three girls sitting on a bench; miniskirts, too much lipstick, and eyes with perfectly curled lashes stare up at me with looks that read, *not so fast*.

"What the fuck could you possibly be coming to see him for? We've had literally one class. How could you already need office hours?"

"The same reason *you're* here?" one sneers and gives me a look that says, *don't bullshit us*. I resist the urge to snap that they are definitely *not* here for the same reason but my good sense takes over and warns me to keep the fuck quiet before I get Aidan fired and myself kicked out of school.

"Right," I tell them. I turn to leave when the door opens and I hear a girl's voice.

"Thank you *so* much, Doctor Reed. I so appreciate it." She giggles and I roll my eyes. I don't even want to watch this scene unfold when I hear my name.

"Miss Mitchell?"

I let out a sigh and turn around. "You know, I can just email you." I shake my head and point towards the line. "I don't have time to wait in line." The words come out bitchier than I intend and I'm instantly irritated for sounding like a jealous fucking girlfriend.

"You made an appointment, you don't have to wait," he responds before I even have a chance to turn around, and his words affect me more than I expect. *Well, they affect my pussy.*

"Ladies, I'm sorry but office hours are over for the day. I

have them tomorrow from four to six." One by one the girls stand up and shoot me angry looks as they walk by me and I know my face is unreadable. I'm not apologetic or smug. I actually don't know what I feel. "After you," he tells me and I make my way into his office.

"I didn't make an appointment," I tell him as soon as his door is shut and...*locked*. I swallow as I watch him turn the lock and suddenly the office seems five times smaller.

"I know." He moves closer to me and visions of what happened the last time I was in this office begin to swirl around my brain.

"Aidan." My knees buckle slightly as I wonder where this is going.

"Bella." The word is as good as an answer. *Thank God.* "I touched my dick picturing your mouth around it last night."

"Same," I answer immediately. "Well, I mean not...my dick..." I giggle, but his face doesn't even crack a hint of a smile.

His hands wrap around my hips and he lifts me slightly sitting me on his desk. "Spread your legs." I do as he says, my body obeying his commands like it's been trained to do so. "I wrapped those pink panties of yours around my hand and rubbed them on my cock," he whispers against my neck, his tongue darting out and moving up my skin. "I came all over them, grunting your name."

My pussy throbs with need at his words and a whimper leaves my lips. "Doctor Reed." I wasn't expecting the words to come out but as soon as they do, his lips leave my neck and he looks at me.

"Again," he grits out.

"Doctor...Reed." A devious smile plays at the corners of my mouth and he growls as his hand reaches under the turquoise dress that I'd chosen to wear today solely because it reminded me of his eyes.

"I have to see your tits this time."

"Here...?" I squeak.

"I don't give a fuck. Your nipples are so fucking perfect. And they're so pretty when they pebble under my gaze. Your body comes alive when I look at you, Skyler."

"Why do you think that is?" I ask, hoping that he concludes that I'm over pretending that he doesn't affect me.

"This is reckless." He slides the straps of my dress down, revealing a barely-there lace bra. "Anyone could knock and they'd know. They'd know I had you in here, half-naked and *wanting*. They'd smell your pussy." He slides my panties down my legs and lets them drop to the floor. "And then I'd have to kill them because *no one* gets to smell your cunt but me, Skyler. Do you remember what I told you?"

"You don't share?" My voice is weak and quiet, the conviction taken out of it by the feeling of his index finger sliding up and down my slit.

"And?"

"That...I'm yours?" I squeak out.

"Correct."

"But..."

"No buts, Skyler."

"You said we couldn't," I moan when his fingers pinch my clit.

He doesn't say anything, he just continues to rub my clit, his breath heavy on my lips. He pulls me off his desk and pushes my dress down letting it pool at my feet. He reaches behind me, unclasps my bra, and it joins my dress on the floor, leaving me completely naked.

In front of my professor

Smack dab in the middle of his office hours.

He rakes my body from my feet to my eyes and licks his lips. "Fuck," he groans and then he's on me, pushing me back on his desk and pressing his lips to my mound. He eats me like a starving man, and I'm his last meal, leaving no part of me untouched. His hands hold me open with his thumbs as he gives me quick strokes. His tongue is unrelenting and aggressive as he pushes me closer to my orgasm.

"Aidan!" I try to be mindful of the volume of my voice but I can't be too bothered to care as I'm dangling over the edge of the orgasm I was desperate for last night. "Oh my God." My hands find his head as my legs rest on his shoulders, effectively keeping his mouth in place. I pull on his hair as I simultaneously push him harder against me. "Holy shit." I squeeze my eyes shut. I'm not sure what I was expecting when I showed up at his office today. *Was I hoping this would be the result? Fuck yes. Did I expect it? I want to say no. But…was that the truth?*

This is reckless. It is wrong. Taboo even. I'm his nineteen year old student. He's my teacher. He's older. I'm in his office…in the middle of the day. The thoughts make me wetter and I almost pass out from the pleasure that he is inflicting.

I dig my nails into his scalp and I'm seconds from letting go when he stops. I feel air hit my sex that previously had his mouth all over it and I begin to protest at the loss of contact. I look up, my eyes taking a second to focus. "Get on all fours," he orders me.

"On your desk?"

"Yes."

I turn over, my ass in the air when I hear him groan from behind me and his fingernails dig into my ass. "I want to do so fucking much to you."

I bite my lip. "Do all of it," I manage to whimper out just in time to feel his teeth sinking into the flesh of ass. I yelp. It hurts a bit more than I thought it would, but the sting is lessened by his tongue soothing the skin. He moves lower, stroking my clit with his tongue, eating me from behind. I feel goosebumps everywhere, and my body feels like I've stuck my finger in a light socket. Every single one of my nerves stand on end, a delicious feeling inside of me causing my toes to curl. I try my best to anchor myself to the desk as I feel like I'm seconds from floating away. My eyes flutter shut while he continues his reckless assault on my pussy. He pulls away for a second and I cry out at how close I was when I feel wetness between my cheeks and then his finger spreading the moisture around my rosebud. *Holy shit.*

I don't even have the words as I feel like my mind has been wiped clean from everything I've ever known. All I know is this gorgeous man that's giving me pleasure that I can't even fathom in even my most dirty fantasies. His tongue returns to the apex of my thighs as his finger continues to probe my asshole mercilessly. *I'm so close I can taste it.*

I don't think I've ever been this wet. His mouth and my sex create a noise that I've never heard before. *It's loud, wet, aggressive. Delicious.* He's eating me the way one eats ice cream on a hot day. Quick deliberate strokes, the wetness dripping down their chin. It's almost as if he's drinking me.

That's how wet I feel. I'd be humiliated if I wasn't so turned the fuck on.

My hands are curled into fists, my knuckles dragging against the hardness of his desk. It hurts but I can't bring myself to unclench my fists. I'm wound so tight that I know the second I release, I'm going to shatter spectacularly into a million pieces. I open my eyes and I'm not shocked that my vision is blurry. Tears well in my eyes as my body tries to accept the pleasure he's giving me.

I'm going to come…harder than I ever have in my life.

It's right…there. And then it comes. *Hard.* "Fuck!" I scream, not giving a fuck that I'm supposed to be quiet as I push my body back harder onto his face. "Don't stop," I whimper, and his other hand grips my ass hard as the aftershocks move through me. "Aidan!" I cry out. Even when the orgasm wanes I feel his mouth there, still, leaving me lazy kisses, his tongue rubbing long, languid strokes against my folds. I try to move away from him but he grabs my hips, keeping me in place as he begins to work me over again. "Wait…" I whine, knowing that my body can't handle the exertion of another orgasm.

"No," he snarls, and I feel it through every part of my body.

"Please."

"You didn't tell me you were a fucking squirter." The words hang in the air causing my cheeks to flush even further. The truth is, I had no idea that I was. *Fuck.* "I am soaked in your fucking cum," he says slowly, as if he's tasting the words as they leave his lips.

I'm still trying to calm my racing heart and throbbing sex when he pulls me off of his desk. My knees rub against the wood and send pain through my body that I try to ignore. Within seconds I'm straddling him on the black leather couch, his lips attached to mine, the wetness from the lower half of his face rubbing all over me.

He pulls away from me and rubs his lips gently across mine. "I can't stay away from you."

"I don't want you to." I play with his belt between us, and lift myself up, so he can unzip his pants and pull his cock out. I slide down onto him the second the hard rod is in sight and I groan as the blunt tip forces its way inside. I feel so wanton in this moment. I'm completely naked, bouncing on top of this man who is completely clothed, my body wound so tight and desperate for not just my release but his as well. *Is he going to come inside of me this time?*

I feel his lips on my right nipple, suckling and biting the hard bud. My hands play with the hair at the nape of his neck and I twist the strands between my fingers. My pussy squeezes his cock and he lets me go with a pop just as his hands drop to my hips so he can control the speed. I begin to move faster on top of him and just as I feel my body about to release, the sound of a phone ringing pierces the air. I freeze on top of him and though I want to keep going, I wonder if he needs to take it.

He looks up at me and then at the phone before squeezing his eyes shut. "I should take that. I don't want anyone showing up here looking for me." I nod as he pulls himself out of me and makes his way towards his desk to answer his phone.

"Doctor Reed." My body flushes hearing him speak into the phone, and he shoots me a wink as he sees that I'm affected. I thought I'd feel more vulnerable, completely naked and on display for him, but I find myself spreading my legs and reaching between them to touch myself for him.

His eyes darken and his nostrils flare as his tongue darts out to wet his lips. "Right…I forgot." His gaze leaves mine and he turns to face the door, running a hand through his hair. "NO," he snarls into the phone. "I'll—I'll be there in a few." He slams the phone down and looks at me. "You have to go."

I sit up, *now* feeling that vulnerability I wasn't feeling before. "Now? You don't want to…" I look down at my naked body, my sex still tingling from the assault of his cock. "Finish?"

"No, Skyler, I don't," he snaps and I don't know what's

happened in the span of thirty seconds or how bad that phone call was for him to take that tone with me. He picks up my dress from the ground and hands it to me. "Next time, someone could show up here and I won't know what the fuck to do. You're a good fuck, but I'm not going to get fired over getting caught with a student with my pants down."

My lip trembles slightly and my heart lurches in my chest. *A good fuck?* "I was supposed to be in a meeting ten minutes ago, and because you make me lose all reason, I'm late. I can't think straight when I'm around you, Skyler."

I stand up slowly, and struggle to keep my body upright. I'm feeling so many emotions coursing through me, I wonder if I might faint. I pull on my dress with shaky hands and slide my underwear up my legs. I'm worried the second I open my mouth I'm going to lose it, so I keep my lips planted firmly together.

"Skyler," I hear the regret in his tone, but I don't give a fuck. *Fucking dick.*

"No," I tell him firmly, "I'm transferring the fuck out of your class." I don't even wait for a response before I'm out the door slamming it behind me.

Aidan

I AM OFFICIALLY THE FUCKING WORST.

That's the only thing I can think as I sit in the staff meeting for all the criminal justice professors. A meeting for which I was twenty minutes late. I'd hurt Skyler in a panic, thinking that the dean of the school was going to show up at my office and pull me out of her by my hair.

He would then proceed to fire me and black ball me from all the schools in D.C., and that would just be the end to a fucking fantastic year. And who knows what would happen to her? Could they kick her out for getting involved with a teacher? I can still see the sad look in her eyes as she pulled her dress on, not even bothering to put on a bra before she succumbed to the tears I know she was hiding. I can't let her transfer out of my class.

Why the fuck not? You clearly can't be her teacher.

Because then she'll be behind a semester. My particular class is needed before she can take any others in her major, and delaying it a semester would deter her from graduating on time. *Am I that selfish that I would put her in that predicament?*

Probably.

My eyes dart around the room, jumping from person to person who is trying their best not to side-eye the new guy that had no regard for anyone's time by being twenty minutes late.

Being the new guy amongst tenured professors is hard. Being the new guy when you are younger and more advanced in their field makes it even harder.

The meeting ends rather quickly, making me wonder why it was so important that I be here in the first place, and why I couldn't have been emailed the details of what I missed. Then I wouldn't have snapped at Skyler and I wouldn't feel like I'm the motherfucking worst.

I drop my bag the second I get home, heading straight for the refrigerator to grab a beer before I sink like a log on the couch. My stomach turns at the thought of seeing Skyler tomorrow.

If she even shows up.

Later that night, I'm sitting at my desk in my apartment, attempting to prepare for my lecture tomorrow when my phone pings with a text message notification. It manages to pull my attention from the PowerPoint I'd half-heartedly put together that even I think is mind-numbing. I look down and my dick twitches when I see her name flashing across the screen. I stare at it for a second, wondering what would come of her texting me at eleven thirty at night.

Open it, my dick urges me.

Calm the fuck down, she's not going to fuck you again.

I've slid my thumb across the phone before I can convince myself to ignore her message.

Skyler: My advisor wouldn't let me transfer out. Guess you're stuck with me. Oh yeah, also fuck you.

Aidan: I can't say I'm not pleased. This is for the best, you don't want to be behind.
Skyler: Why do you even fucking care? You treated me like complete shit today, don't be nice to me now.
Aidan: Of course I care. Skyler, I'm sorry.
Skyler: This is the second time you've been a dick to me. I can MAYBE give you a pass for the first one because you were caught off guard. But today was bullshit.
Aidan: I know…
Skyler: Well, whatever. I just wanted to let you know that you'd see me tomorrow.
Aidan: I look forward to it.
Skyler: I don't.
Aidan: I'm sorry to hear that.

She doesn't respond despite my staring at the phone, willing her to. It isn't until ten minutes later that my phone vibrates again, indicating a phone call. I don't hesitate to answer.

"Skyler?"

"Hello, it's me. Yes. I mean…hi. Okay, let's get something straight." I hear her slur and now I understand the reasons for her texts and her calls. She clears her throat. "We are not having sex ever again."

I grit my teeth and the words taste awful coming out of my mouth. My dick strains against my sweats hearing her words as cum pools at the tip. "I know."

"Even though you are great at it."

I lean back in my chair, a smug grin finding my face that I'm glad she can't see. "Is that so?"

"Yes. Really good. But I have to move on. *La vita va Avanti*, remember?"

I nod. She doesn't sound all that sure of that affirmation,

but I chalk it up to the alcohol coursing through her system. "I remember."

"So, you're…the past. Not the future." I hear her talking to someone. "No, go away, Peyton." She snorts. "I'm not going to tell him that." I strain to listen, wondering what Peyton advised her to tell me. "Because!" *Silence.* "Peyton wants me to tell you, that I am hot and I will find another guy that appreciates me." I hear more shuffling. "What? That's what you said!"

I'm not mad that I've been drunk dialed by this college student who isn't even legally old enough to drink. I'm mad that she mentioned herself with another guy. *No one better fucking touch her.*

"Skyler, where are you?"

"At a bar." She giggles. "Using my fake ID."

"I wish you'd stop that shit."

"Well…that's not your call, now is it?"

"Which bar?"

"What…you're going to come here? I wouldn't if I were you. This place is crawling with college students. One might recognize ya."

"I'll risk it. Now tell me," I order.

⁂

With a Boston Red Sox hat pulled low over my head, a Harvard t-shirt and jeans, I look like I may just pass for a college student. *Or hell, at least someone under the age of thirty.* I pull up to the bar, and make my way inside, grateful that I don't have to wait in a line too long. The bar is massive, way bigger than *Lush* and I find myself wondering how the hell I'm going to find her in the sea of people that are already heavily intoxicated. The bar is packed causing people to filter out onto the patio that is lit by twinkling lights. The bass thumps in my ears and vibrates through my system as I watch students enjoy their time before the semester really starts and going out on a Tuesday night becomes a distant memory. I make my way through the crowd and my ears immediately perk up when I hear a high pitched squeal followed by "Sky!" I whip my head towards the source of the sound and my eyes almost pop out of my head when I see Skyler.

Fuck. Me.

She's wearing a black crop top that shows far too much skin, both cleavage and midriff with a long skirt that stops just above her ankles. She has on heels that give her a little bit of height and her hair is off her shoulders in a sexy bun that I want to pull on as I fuck her from behind. *She looked hot as fuck.* My eyes move behind her to see that she is dancing with some douche in a polo and boat shoes whose hands are secured around her waist as she shakes her ass against him. Her hands raise up every few seconds, her hips swaying to the beat and revealing even more of her tan torso. *A torso I'd had my mouth all over no more than five hours ago. Fuck that.*

The reasonable side of me urges that I hang back and wait to make sure that said guy isn't a student at CGU. Or at least until she finishes dancing with him so that I don't embarrass her.

But the other side, a much stronger more overbearing side, roars that no one can touch Skyler. That she's mine and that fucker doesn't know who he's messing with.

I push through the crowd before my reasonable side can stop me until I'm standing in front of her, my hat low, and staring her down. Our eyes lock and her breath hitches, almost as if she doesn't recognize me yet. I grab her shoulders and pull her towards me, out of the grip of the guy behind her and realization must dawn on her because she gasps. Her teeth find her bottom lip but other than that she doesn't react. "Aidan," she mouths.

"What the fuck dude, we were dancing," the guy says to me, but I don't look at him. I don't even acknowledge him as I lead her away. My hand slides around her shoulder possessively.

"And now you're not."

"What the fuck?"

"She was using you to make me jealous. Get over it," I call over my shoulder. I'm not sure if he heard me, but I'm positively sure I don't care.

"Are you?" she asks as she looks up at me.

"Am I what?" I pull her out of the crowd, into a less crowded area, and pull her into my arms. Her skin is soft and I want to run my hands over every inch of her.

"Jealous?"

Yes. "What do you think?" She nods her head and I lean down to press my lips to the space behind her ear. "We've already been over that. I don't share."

"But you don't want me at all."

"I never said that."

"You said I'm a good fuck but you don't want to get fired over it."

I wince, hearing the brutal words thrown back at me. I regretted it the second I said it. "You're more than a good fuck, Skyler. You know that."

"I don't know anything. And quite frankly, for thirty-two, you act like a fucking college fuckboy. Say what you mean and mean what you say." She crosses her arms in front of her and I don't miss the glaze in her eye, making me remember that she'd had more than a little bit to drink tonight.

"Fair. I shouldn't have said that. I'm sorry. I'm a bit out

of my depth navigating a relationship with someone I can't have."

"Relationship?"

"Whatever you want to call this." I rub a hand behind my head. "How much have you had to drink, Skyler?" She swallows and looks around, shifting nervously from one foot to the other. "Answer me," I order her.

"Like one or two?" She puts her two fingers up innocently and holds them next to her cheek.

"Bullshit. You can barely focus your eyes," I growl at her and she frowns.

"What do you even care? You're not my father. You're not my boyfriend. Just leave me alone, Aidan." She backs up slightly and I wonder if she's going to leave, but I don't give her the option as I grab her hand.

"You don't think I want to!?" I raise my voice louder than I intend but it isn't enough to alert anyone given the volume of the music. I pull my hat down lower over my eyes and glower at the drunk but unbelievably pretty girl swaying against me. "I'm taking you home."

"With you?" she squeaks and I don't miss the way my cock twitches at the thought of her writhing underneath me.

"Yes, but we're not doing anything."

You sure about that?

Skyler's heels are off her feet before I've even shut the door of my apartment, and she turns around in the space. Never in a million years did I think I would ever have a drunk college student in my apartment at one in the morning.

But then again, I never saw Skyler coming.

"Your place is cute!" She peeks her head around the kitchen and living room before turning to look at me. "Can I see your bedroom?"

I swallow hard, my Adam's apple bobbing in my throat as I try to hold on to some shred of control so that I don't end up taking this drunk nineteen year old on my kitchen counter. I'm old enough to know better.

But I may have been just young enough not to care.

"Skyler..." I trail off as I pull my hat off and toss it on the counter. "We can't have sex."

"And why not?"

"Well, for starters, because you said you weren't having sex with me anymore."

She twists her face into a sexy pout and stares at the ceiling as if she's trying to recall saying that. "That wasn't me."

"Oh? You sure? Because...I have the texts."

"Nope. No idea who that was." She walks towards my fridge and opens it like she owns the place. "Ooh beer!" She pulls one out and pops it open before I have a chance to stop her.

"Skyler, baby, you've had enough."

"Did you just call me...?" She pulls the can out of my reach and backs up. "So, I'm baby again?"

I ignore her comment. The word had slipped out of my mouth so casually, as if I've been saying it for years. "Can I have the beer?" I hold my hand out, wanting to stop her from drinking anymore and adding to the hangover I know she will have tomorrow.

She takes a long gulp of it and hands it to me. I sigh when I realize it's half empty. "Skyler, you have class in the morning. We should get some sleep." I'm expecting an argument, but I start to see the exhaustion setting in all over her face. She lets out a sigh and pulls her hair from the bun, letting it fall to her shoulders in sexy waves.

"I assume you don't have any makeup wipes?" she asks me. Her eyes have started to droop and she rubs at them, smearing her mascara under her eyes.

"Afraid not." I lead her down the hall towards my bedroom, holding her small hand in mine and wishing it was wrapped around my dick instead.

"An extra toothbrush?" she asks and I shake my head. She sits on my bed just before sending her skirt down her legs and leaving her in her crop top and a pair of underwear that look more like dental floss. I'm hanging on by an actual thread at this point, so I immediately move to my dresser and pull a pair of sweatpants out of a drawer for her to wear. I turn around and I see that she's disappeared into my bathroom.

I let out the breath I realize I've been holding. *Aidan, keep your hands to your fucking self.* I rub my jaw, wondering if maybe I should just sleep on the couch so that I'm not tempted to touch her where I know I shouldn't.

What if she wakes up tomorrow and she's pissed to be in bed with you?

My thoughts are interrupted by Skyler's fresh face moving through my bedroom in nothing more than her panties and a strapless bra. I cough, trying to hide the groan that is sitting in the back of my throat. I shift away from her so that I can inconspicuously readjust my dick, and Skyler bounces on the bed.

"It's been a while since I washed my face with just plain soap and water. I used some of your mouthwash... I was going to use your toothbrush, but I don't think we're there yet," she rambles before laying back on my bed and snuggling underneath my covers. "It's cold in here."

"I got you a pair of sweatpants."

She shakes her head and lets her eyes flutter closed as a yawn leaves her lips. "Come snuggle me, that will warm me up."

"Skyler…" I warn.

"Just to keep me warm."

"I'm onto you, Skyler," I tell her.

"Mmm, not yet." She giggles, but her eyes are still closed. She submerges her face in my pillows and pulls the blankets up to her neck. "Thank you for coming to get me, Aidan," she whispers.

"You're welcome, Skyler. Hey, what time is your first class tomorrow morning?" I don't want her missing class because she's laid up in her professor's bed, hungover. *And I can't be here next to her, cuddling her.*

"Ummm ten?" I can tell sleep is going to find her any second so I turn the light out, sheathing the room in darkness.

I press a kiss to her forehead followed by her cheek before I go into the bathroom to do a few things.

Mainly jack off.

Skyler

I wake up the next morning to the roar of the pounding in my temples. I put a hand over my forehead and groan. I'm surprised to hear a chuckle close by. I move my hand and have to blink a few times in order to convince my brain that they aren't playing tricks on me. Aidan is sitting next to me, shirtless, holding a cup of coffee in his hands. "Good morning, princess."

"What the…what time is it?"

"A little after seven."

I groan at the early hour. "What the fuck? I'm going back to sleep." *If my memory serves me correctly, I don't have class until ten, which means I don't need to be fully functioning until nine at the earliest.*

"I made you some coffee."

"And that's all well and good, but I'm still going back to sleep."

"You sure?" he asks and I open one eye. I will admit that he is just as gorgeous as I remember without a shirt. The bed creaks. I see him get up and walk around the bed to my side where he sits next to me, and only then do I realize he is *completely naked*.

"Fuck." I let out a breath and sit up slightly, holding my hands out for him to hand me the cup. "Did we? We didn't last night, right?"

"We didn't."

I take a sip of my coffee and eye him warily. "Why?"

"Because you were pretty drunk. And I wasn't sure you wanted to."

"I wanted to." The last of the alcohol still swirling around my brain is making me bold and I don't care. *I wanted him. I will always want him.*

But this back and forth is getting exhausting. Honestly, he's giving me whiplash.

"I don't want to hurt you again, Skyler."

"Then… don't." I know it isn't that simple, but I've come to realize that I want a relationship with a man that *is* that simple. Maybe Aidan isn't that man. Yet here I am anyway, laying my cards on the table.

I had prepared to let a man into my bed, but I'm shocked at how quick I've let someone into my heart again. The past two days I had been all out of sorts over a man that is supposed to be a quick fuck to *clear out the cobwebs,* as Peyton so eloquently put it. Somewhere between getting in and getting out, I got stuck. The wounds from my prior relationship haven't completely healed, and yet here I am opening myself up to a man that only has the power to hurt me.

Where is this even going?

He already said he can't do this, but then he came to get me, and I'm in his bed. What the fuck does this man even want?

And more importantly, do I want it?

He's silent, and I assume my words pleading with him not to hurt me hit him harder than I intended. He takes my coffee from my hands and sets the mug on the nightstand. He reaches for me and I shrink away from his touch, backing away slowly, and frown. "You can't keep jerking me around, Aidan. I know this is risky, but it is for me too and I'm willing to take the risk. Are you?"

He moves closer to me and pulls me towards him, resting his forehead against mine. "Skyler," he whispers, and his breath hits my lips gently. He cups my face and makes our eyes lock. *"Mi dispiace, dolcezza."* His words send a tremor through me, igniting a spark and warming the space between my legs. *I'm sorry, sweetheart.*

I bite my lip to prevent the whimper from leaving my lips. "You can't use Italian to seduce me, Aidan." *Yes, he can.*

"Per favore." Please.

"Aidan…" I trail off and he weaves his fingers into my hair. He rubs my ears gently and draws a trail with his lips all over my face, kissing my cheeks, forehead, and nose, completely avoiding my lips.

"Sono pazzo di te." I'm crazy about you.

I push him back, knowing that between the kisses and his Italian I can't think straight. "Aidan. Stop. Use words."

"I am," he whispers. *"Non voglio che finisca."* I don't want this to end.

"Could have fooled me. You ended it, Aidan." I pull out of his grasp and raise an eyebrow at him. He doesn't say anything at first. His eyes leave my face briefly and I can see the wheels turning in that mind of his before he turns his gaze back to me.

"I want this, but…we have to be careful."

I don't say anything, and he must take as me being more receptive for him to touch me because he pulls me into his naked lap and presses a hot kiss to my chest, bare except for the tiny strapless bra. I have vague memories of getting undressed in his bathroom last night with the intention to seduce him, but I guess that didn't pan out.

He unsnaps my bra behind me and I shiver at his cool hands touching my body, still warm from being snuggled under his blankets. I lean forward and drag my nose against his. "I think I can be careful."

"Can you? You were pretty reckless last night, Skyler." He pauses. "I didn't like it."

"I was just out with my friends. People party in college. It's what college kids do."

He grabs my jaw and squeezes. "I'm not always going to be around to keep you safe, Skyler. Keep your ass out of trouble and more importantly other guys' hands off of you. I mean it."

"Yes, sir." My skin hums along with the purr that leaves my lips. I rub my nose along his jaw and press my naked chest into his. I'm not sure how I feel about all of this, but I am sure

I want him inside of me…*now.* Especially since I know he's no longer a flight risk. I can figure out my feelings later. "Are you going to fuck me now?"

His hands are in my hair and then around my back. He moves them to the space right above my ass and plucks at the thong tucked between my ass cheeks. "Lay back," he breathes in my ear and I don't wait a second before I do what he says, pulling my underwear off at the same time.

"As much as I love feeling the wet flesh of your bare pussy, we are using a condom. We're playing with fire." He tells me as he presses a finger into my sex and begins rubbing against my clit. It had been less than twenty-four hours since I felt him inside me and my body is already starting to build with the painful need to come around him. I stretch my feet, pointing my toes hard, feeling them curl and extend in preparation for my climax.

"Aidan, fuck me, please."

"Not yet." He pulls his fingers out of me and before I have a chance to react to the loss of contact, his mouth is on me. His tongue penetrates my wet channel, rubbing my inner walls before pulling out of me and flicking my clit. He does that motion again and again until he settles on my clit, alternating between licking, sucking, and nibbling. I've never felt teeth on my clit until Aidan, and I realize it is something I like. *Not hard.* Just a gentle graze that sends delicious jolts up my spine and into my brain. My body sizzles under his mouth and I want nothing more than to watch it move later today in class, knowing that this morning he'd had it all over me.

It would take everything out of me not to shoot the girls in my class a look that said: *that man is mine.*

I grip the back of his head and clamp my thighs around his ears as I watch him submerge his entire face in my sex.

The tip of his tongue continues to tickle the engorged flesh between my legs and I'm ready to explode. "Fuck, Aidan. I'm going to come!"

I hear him slurping and sucking everything that my body offers him. "Come, Skyler. I know you're close."

I begin to rock against his face, feeling the orgasm at the tip of my tongue…*and his as well*. "Yes!" I scream. "Oh my God, Oh my God, Oh my Goddddd," I chant. I shut my eyes just as the feeling explodes through me, causing fireworks behind my eyelids. I'm barely down from the high when he's inside of me, pounding into me mercilessly and tapping my G-spot every few strokes.

This man is an actual sex God.

His strokes slow, and his lips find mine as we begin the sensual dance that matches what our lower halves are doing. I've known Aidan three days and already he knows the language of my soul. "Fuck, Skyler. *La mia bellissima ragazza,*" he whispers in my ear and I shiver. *My beautiful girl.* His hands tighten on my hips and then my legs are up next to my ears, my ankles just above my head as he continues his reckless assault on my pussy. I look up at him, and his intense gaze takes my breath away. His dark blue eyes penetrate me as deep as his cock, and I can't handle the physical and emotional sensations. I shut my eyes, needing to break the connection on some level, and knowing I can't tell him to stop.

My heart thumps wildly in my chest, banging against my ribcage with every thrust. Aidan is turning me inside out, slowly. I just hope my heart will be intact when I come out on the other side.

Skyler

One month later

I TAP MY PEN AGAINST MY TEETH, A SMILE FINDING MY LIPS AS I watch Aidan try to avoid my gaze. I bite down on the lid, running my tongue along it every few seconds. I manage to catch his gaze and before he can break our eye contact I lick my lips. He swallows, but doesn't miss a beat. I guess after thirty days of my torture, he's gotten rather immune to it. The first week, he barely kept it together as I constantly teased him all class. I'd played with my hair, made a show of taking my jacket off and even got up to go to the bathroom, which led to a full thirty seconds of silence as I know he followed my ass with his eyes as I left the room.

We'd been good though. We hadn't been to his office again since that second day, although we had graced a stairwell in the law library...*twice*.

For the most part though, we kept things to his place or my place after class hours. I'd spent the better part of the last month falling asleep wrapped up in Aidan Reed's arms, and I can't stop the feeling that I'm falling hard for him.

But what future can you have? Where is this all going?

A part of me wonders if he is even interested in getting more serious once the semester is over and I'm no longer his student. I want to ask, but I'm honestly too nervous to hear his reply.

What if this is all just fun for him?

I know he had a bitchy ex-fiancée who clearly didn't appreciate him. She'd hurt him. Destroyed him to the point that he wasn't sure if he could do it again. The hurt he endured, and the pain he is still obviously in, slices through me, making me wonder if we are more alike than I thought.

I thought maybe I had been unreasonable about what had happened with Gabriel, but hearing Aidan talk about his ex-fiancée, made me realize that you can't put an age on heartbreak. *Feelings are beyond reason.*

I must have missed hearing him dismiss class early because people are getting up around me and clearing out of the classroom. Per usual, there's a line of girls waiting to talk to him and I know this is one of the days I can't stay and wait. We'd come up with a schedule, so that it doesn't become obvious that we have an unorthodox relationship for a student and a professor. Sometimes I can wait to talk to him and other times I have to go. I pout as I think about how this is one of those times I have to go.

My phone buzzes and I assume it's Peyton asking if I can meet up for lunch. *"Or if I was going somewhere to have Aidan's dick for lunch."* Peyton's words.

Aidan: I want to bend you over this desk and explore your cunt with my mouth.

My eyes widen and I almost drop my phone seeing his

explicit words on the screen. I go to respond when I get another message.

Aidan: And then I want you to do to my cock what you were doing to that pen all Goddamn class. Never have I ever wanted to be a fucking ballpoint so badly.

I look up to see him typing on his computer, while a girl yammers on about some stupid bullshit. *"Help me with my paper, I think I need extra help, please let me suck your dick?"* I swear I can hear it as clear as day as I watch the pretty brunette from the third row twirl her hair nervously.

Aidan: Stop looking jealous.

I actually grunt at my phone and shoot him a glare that I know he doesn't see, but can *feel*.

Aidan: Meet me at my office. Five minutes.
Skyler: We said no more sex in your office.
Aidan: That was before I saw you in a pair of leggings.
Skyler: I can come over later?
Aidan: Skyler. My office.
Skyler: No, it's risky. Later. I'll leave the leggings on. *kissy face*

I don't wait for a reply before heading out of the door, knowing that he won't stop me.

I spot Peyton on the quad in her usual spot, typing away on her computer, and I wonder if she's finished her philosophy paper.

"Hey, P."

"Ah, I was wondering when you'd show up. Afternoon delight?" She giggles, and I roll my eyes. Every day she asks if we had sex and every day I tell her no.

"He's coming over later."

"So lame." She pouts. "You hardly ever come out anymore." She shoots me a look and rolls her eyes. "I know his dick game is amazing, but really, Sky?"

"I know. I know." I lower my head in shame at becoming one of those girls that spends all her free time with her boyfriend. "I just…I can't very well bring him out with me, now can I? I can't even bring him to your pregames." I pause, knowing that Peyton isn't going to let this go. "But maybe you could come over?" I shrug non-committedly. I'm not sure how that would go over with Aidan even though he knows Peyton knows our secret. "I think Chace might be coming back to town soon." A smile finds her lips and her eyebrows almost shoot up to her hairline.

"Reallyyyyy," she says dramatically. "Hot Chace? Chace who may or may not have appeared during one or two of my shower orgasms?"

"Didn't need to know that?" I shake my head as I pull the protein bar out of my bag that Aidan had all but shoved into my hands when we left this morning. Usually he cooks breakfast for me, but this morning we couldn't get out of bed for anything, which also made me five minutes late for my first class.

"When's he coming?" she asks, a twinkle in her blue eyes alerting me that she would definitely not let him slip through her fingers this time.

"Aidan said maybe next weekend."

"I will make myself way available for the occasion." She raises an eyebrow at me before I see her pulling her phone out.

I almost choke on my food when I hear her next words. "Hi, I'm calling to see if I can book an appointment for a Brazilian wax next week?"

The smell of lasagna wafts around me and my mouth waters, giving me feelings of nostalgia and reminding me of home. I look up from my computer and watch Aidan move around his kitchen. His arms flex and tighten as he does something so domestic. *For me.* And in nothing more than a pair of sweatpants that make my mouth water and a t-shirt. Aidan Reed, also known as the most gorgeous man I'd ever met and the best sex of my life, is now making me dinner.

I am so fucked.

He catches me staring and shoots me a grin that I feel deep in my core. My heart flutters and I try to stop myself from going deep into the fantasy of this similar scenario in five years, ten years, fifty years.

Yep, I'm in deep.

"Do you need help?" I ask.

"Nope, you stay there and study."

"You know I'm going to be a tough critic. I *am* Italian. Marinara is in my veins."

"I know. I told myself I wanted to cook you something I knew you'd love and were familiar with, but now I'm shitting myself thinking you won't like it."

I stand up and make my way over to the kitchen where I wrap my arms around him. "I was just kidding. I'm sure I'll love it because you made it and no man has ever cooked me dinner before."

He leans down and presses his mouth to mine, sliding

his tongue through my lips, letting me taste the wine that he wouldn't let me have *"until your homework is done"*. I look at his counter and see all of the necessary ingredients, and I run through a mental checklist. "Seasoning is half the battle. You remembered parsley?"

"Yes."

"Basil?"

"Yes, Skyler." I can sense the exasperation in his voice.

I put my hands up. "Okay, just checking. Smells good." I reach for his wine glass and take a tentative sip.

"Is your homework done?"

I give him a cheeky grin. "I don't know...want to check it?"

He raises an eyebrow at me. "What are you working on?"

"Work for your class. Although, I don't know why. Sleeping with the professor should have *some* perks." I giggle as I make my way back to the table and sit with his wine glass in hand, letting the flavors of the Malbec take me back to my Italian vacation.

"Is that so?" He moves across the room and leans over me. "You think I should just *give* you an A because we're sleeping together?"

"Of course not." I flutter my eyelashes and let my tongue dart out and lick a drop of stray wine. "I think you should give me an A because I give fantastic head and I let you stick your dick in my ass."

His nostrils flare and I watch him rub his hands together like he's preparing for something *sinful*. "Fantastic head, huh?"

"Mmmhmm." I turn back to my computer, knowing full well that I'm about to be taking a very long study break. He tugs on my bun, letting it fall from the confines of my ponytail holder and makes me look up at him.

"We'll circle back to my dick in your ass later. Do you think your blow jobs warrant you an A, Miss Mitchell?"

"I know they do," I quip.

"So, you'd be willing to bet your entire grade on an oral exam, then?" His face leans down and it's so close I can almost taste it.

"Absolutely."

"Prove it."

I'm kneeling between Aidan's legs as he sits in the chair in his living room that I swear is only meant for old men to take naps in. My hands are on his naked thighs as he runs his hand up and down his cock. "Do you want this, Miss Mitchell?" he asks and I move forward slightly when he puts a hand over my mouth. "Beg for it."

"*You* beg for it," I bite back playfully.

"Ah ah, you're the one that wants the A." I huff like a defiant child not getting her way. "Ask me."

"To what," I whisper.

"Ask me to let you suck my dick."

I narrow my eyes at him, doing my best to play the part of the bratty school girl. *God knows I would beg for anything he wanted me to.* "Please, Doctor Reed." I bite down on my bottom lip for emphasis and look up at him through my eyelashes. I tuck a hair behind my ear nervously and look away from his piercing gaze. "My parents are used to seeing me get straight A's. They'll freak."

"Hmmm." He taps his chin as he continues to pull on his dick. "Do I get to come in that pretty little mouth of yours?"

"If...if that's what you want?"

"Good answer." He grunts as I assume he's getting himself closer to the edge with no help from me.

"Do you need a hand with that?" I purse my lips and stare up into his eyes.

"I need your mouth on it."

"And then I get an A?"

"And then you get an A, princess." His eyes are dark, his lips are parted, and I can see his tongue running along his teeth. *He's ready to explode.*

"Okay...I—I've never done this before," I whisper, breathily.

"I'll teach you." He nods as he lets go and my hand takes over, slowly moving up and down his steel rod. "Lick the tip, baby." And I do. He rewards me with a deep and guttural groan. "Fuck," he hisses as he leans his head back and shuts his eyes. I lick his tip again and he twitches before I sheath my entire mouth around him and push him to the back of my throat. "God damn, your mouth, Skyler." Both of his hands are in my hair as he pushes up and into my mouth. His grip on my hair tightens and I respond by digging my nails into his thighs. I let him fall from my mouth with a pop and trail my tongue up the underside of his shaft. I look up at him just as I put him back into my mouth and he's staring at me through hooded slits. "Skyler."

"Doctor Reed," I mumble around his cock.

"Make me come and you get an A."

Spurred on by his words, I push myself, desperate to get him to the finish line. I suck and slurp, moaning and letting out little whimpers that I know drive him wild. "Sky," he groans and then his cock expands in my mouth and his orgasm begins. He shudders underneath me as his salty liquid slides down my throat. I continue to suck long after he's done giving me all that he has to offer before letting him slide from between my lips. I go to sit back on my heels when he lifts me up and settles me on his naked cock, making me straddle him. I'm wearing my underwear and a t-shirt without a bra, and my nipples are hardening, poking against the cotton.

"Did I get the A?" I ask.

"You get whatever you fucking want, Miss Mitchell." He shakes his head and gives me a smile. *"Ti penso ogni giorno."* *I think about you every day.*

"I swear you speak better Italian than I do." I giggle and he smiles but it doesn't reach his eyes.

"I'm serious, Skyler." He rubs his face and swallows. "I wasn't…I mean this wasn't supposed to be…" He looks around the room. *"Sei la luce della mia vita."* *You are the light of my life.*

"Me?" His words circle around me before burrowing their way into my heart. *Is he feeling what I'm feeling? Is he falling for me as hard as I'm falling for him?*

"You, Skyler."

I take a breath, steeling myself for a potentially uncomfortable conversation. "What does…what does all *this* mean?"

"I don't know." He licks his lips and I yearn to run my tongue over the same trail, but I think we need to have this conversation. "I think it means that this is real for me," he murmurs quietly. *"We* are real."

I can't stop the smile from blossoming across my face. "Me too." My words are soft and timid but they're there, and now that our words are in the atmosphere there's no turning back.

"You and me," he whispers against my lips.

"You and me," I whisper back as he lifts me into his arms and carries me to his bedroom.

After two rounds of sex, we decide to take a break to eat and for me to *actually* do my homework for his class. I'm not sure if Aidan will give me anything lower than an A, but I figure I should still give him work that *warrants* one. A few hours later, I'm in his bed highlighting a line in my textbook that I've reread at least six times when I feel his eyes on me. I look at him out of the corner of my eye before turning towards him slowly. "Can I help you?"

"You know you can." He rests his lips against my shoulder before kissing it.

"I want to, but I have to do this. In theory, maybe I can bomb *your* quizzes, but not these other ones."

"You won't bomb, you're brilliant."

I beam under his praise, my cheeks heating as I shoot him a smile. "Thank you, but I really do need to study." I turn back to my book.

"Fine, you read, and I'll do something else to keep me occupied."

I wave him off and no more than thirty seconds later do I feel hands wrapping around my legs spreading them slightly. "What the..." I move my textbook to see Aidan lying between my legs, his face descending between them. "Aidannnn," I whine.

"*Whattt...*" His whine matches mine. "Just a little taste, and then I'll leave you alone, I swear."

I raise an eyebrow at him knowing that a little taste will turn into another round of sex and another hour I've spent not getting anything done. "Aidan Reed, you stay away from me when midterms roll around, I mean it." I toss my book to the side and let him pull me down the bed before ripping my underwear from me and pressing his lips to the space that is aching for his kiss.

Aidan

I STARE UP INTO THE CROWD OF THE SIXTY STUDENTS IN MY Social Justice 101 lecture, trying my best to keep my eyes off of one student in particular. I thought maybe it wouldn't be so bad having Skyler in my class, but it's become my own personal hell. When she's not teasing the fuck out of me, she's blowing me away with her insight. I thought maybe she'd lie low and avoid speaking in class, but *nope,* she has an answer for fucking everything, and they are always well thought out and concise. Frankly, I don't know if the teasing or her arguments make me harder.

"Now, not to sound like anyone's *Dad,*" I hear a few groans and even more chuckles, "but I know it's Halloween this weekend, and I just want to make sure everyone is safe. So... yeah," I laugh, "don't do anything I wouldn't do? Which isn't much. But...just don't get yourselves thrown in jail or die. Sound good?" Everyone laughs and I snap my fingers. "Oh, I have your papers." And I grin, knowing that they were hoping that they could get by without having to see some of their terrible grades.

Truly, some of these papers were garbage.

"I will allow rewrites," I continue. "Just shoot me an email and we can talk about it. My door is open." I begin dropping their papers on their desks, and a smile finds my lips when I smell the familiar perfume swirling around me as I approach Skyler. I shoot her a smile and she returns it. I set her paper in front of her before moving on to the rest of the class. Once I'm finished, I move to the front of the room. "Everyone enjoy your weekend, and I'll see you Monday." I watch as the students get up and begin to file their way out of the classroom. Most of the girls that usually stay and flirt with me at the end of class have already left, making me wonder if Halloween festivities kick off earlier than when I was in college.

I try to ignore her, but I see one student still planted firmly in her seat, staring down at her paper and I already know what's coming; I can feel the tension radiating off of her. I know her body better than she does and *she. is. pissed.* I try to stifle the chuckle as she waits for the entire class to file out before she looks up at me and gives me a look that could kill. I'm not sure what she's going to do, but I'm prepared for just about everything as she stomps over to my desk.

"What the fuck is this, Aidan?" she growls at me and I steeple my fingers under my chin.

"Excuse me, Miss Mitchell? Is that any way to talk to your professor?"

"Oh, pardon. What the fuck is this, *Doctor Reed*?" she sasses, and I can tell that she's not in the mood. I'm going to enjoy fucking with her just a little longer.

"What's wrong?"

"What's wrong?! Cut the shit, this isn't funny. In what world does this paper deserve an F? I've never even gotten an F before." She opens her paper past the cover page. "What is this anyway? My theory was unresearched? Aidan, you asked for twelve sources, I gave you twenty, what the fuck more research do you want?"

"Language, Miss Mitchell." I don't know how she hasn't been able to tell that I was just messing with her, that her real paper is tucked in my briefcase. I had actually thought her paper was brilliant and by far the best in the class.

"Really?" She stomps her foot. "Change my fucking grade, right now, or I'm never blowing you again."

"Wow. That is a big threat." I chuckle. "But really, I have to give you the grade I think you deserve."

"You can't be serious!" she shrieks and slams her hand down on my desk. "This is bullshit!"

I chuckle, knowing that she's probably meeting Peyton for lunch so I need to wrap this up before she storms out of here and remains mad at me for the rest of the day. "Skyler," I stand up. "The F stands for *fuck*. As in, I cannot wait to *fuck* you all over every surface of my apartment later."

"You better not bring your dick anywhere near me if you want it to remain attached to your damn body."

I wince and shield my balls that almost jump back up for protection. "Ouch, Sky. Is that any way to talk to the man that made you come four times last night? *And* twice this morning?"

She takes a step back and frowns. "I'm mad at you, don't try and seduce me."

"Baby," I chuckle, "this isn't your real paper." I shake my head before reaching into my briefcase. "*This* is your real paper." I watch as she looks at the new paper and the bright red A on the front page. "You might be the best sex of my life but you're also the brightest student I've ever encountered. Your paper was phenomenal, Skyler."

Her eyes flit up to mine and a smile plays at her lips.

"Really?" Her eyes are bright and full of wonder, and for the first time in a while I'm reminded of her age.

She's nineteen. I'm thirty-two.

It doesn't seem like a huge difference, and maybe one day it wouldn't be, but right now it feels *huge*.

One day.

The words blare in my head like a neon light.

I swallow and shake the wayward thoughts, knowing that nothing is going to keep me from her, especially not our age gap.

"Really. If I thought I could keep my hands off of you long enough for us to get any work done, I'd hire you as a research assistant." She smiles brightly and I shake my head. "No, Skyler."

"Fine," she grumbles. "But no one from your fan club either."

"My fan club?"

"You know who. The group of girls that swarm you after every class and beg for your attention." She puts both of her papers in her bag and hoists it over her shoulder.

"Hmmm, so are you the president of this fan club?"

"Ugh." She scoffs. "I am not in your fan club."

"You're not? You're not a fan of me?" I try my best to look affronted. "You're certainly a fan of my dick."

She snorts and rolls her eyes. "Sometimes I forget you're not my age, you know that?"

I laugh and we fall into step as we leave my classroom. "Are you meeting Peyton? Can I walk you to the quad?"

"Yes, please." And I'm pleased with how giddy she gets just by offering to walk with her. It isn't something we can do every day, and we can't hold hands or be affectionate, but we can talk and be in each other's company, and it thrills us both. We are almost out of the law building when I hear my name being called.

I turn around to see the dean of the school, Doctor Hendricks coming towards us. "Miss Mitchell, we can discuss your paper another time."

"Of course, Doctor Reed. Thank you again." She nods in understanding.

"I'll see you on Monday," I tell her before she waves at me and turns to jog down the stairs. It takes everything out of me to pull my gaze from her and not watch her until she disappears out of sight, but I remember I have an audience. "Doctor Hendricks, how's it going, sir?"

"Well, thank you. How are you settling in?"

"Great. It seems all my students like me."

"Mmmhmm, I'll bet." Doctor Hendricks is old enough to be my father, with white hair that he always keeps slicked down. He wears tweed suits with pocket squares and bow ties and everything about him screams cliché, down to his loafers. A handlebar mustache that matches his hair sits proudly on his upper lip and sometimes he even twirls it as if he's in a movie. *He'd be comical if he weren't such a fucking nuisance.* "Walk with me, son."

I walk next to him and I can see he's struggling with how to start. "Some of the other professors are just a bit—concerned with how *casual* you are with your students."

"Casual?"

"Yes. They've seen that you have quite a large *following*, typically congregated outside of your door during your office hours. They also stay after class. A group of the…female persuasion lined up to talk to you about…"

"The class?"

He looks at me. "Don't be daft, now."

"I don't know what you're implying, *Joe*." *Whatever it is, I could go to HR with it.*

Careful now, Aidan. What he's implying, is what you ARE actually doing.

"I'm not the enemy here. I'm just trying to keep you out of trouble. We've had young professors before. Tale as old as time, son. Young professor. Students. The line becomes blurry, yadda yadda yadda." He puts his hand on my shoulder and squeezes. "I just don't want you to get into trouble. Engaging with a student in an inappropriate manner is grounds for immediate dismissal. God, and the scandal it would cause. I just want you to make sure that you are keeping the lines clear with all students."

My heart pounds harder for a few beats, but I manage to get it under control as I reassure myself that Skyler and I aren't going to get caught. We have a system and we stick to it. "Dr. Hendricks, I can assure you, all of my students know where that line is. I've never given anyone any indication otherwise."

I hear the qualifications in my lie even as I speak them. *I met Skyler before she was a student. And she knows exactly where that line is.*

We can't fuck in my office.

We can't kiss in class.

And she can't take her tests while sitting in my lap.

Other than that, I gave her free reign of "the line."

"Well, that's good to know, son. I would hate for you to allow your hormones to jeopardize your future here at Camden Graf."

I bite my tongue, resisting the urge to tell him where he could stick his unsolicited and somewhat offensive advice. *Do I seem like the guy that would get himself wrapped up in some shit like that?*

Regardless of the fact that I am that guy, do I seem like I *need* this lecture?

FIRST *Semester*

I spot Skyler immediately on the quad, my eyes trained to find her in any crowd. I hang back, mulling over Doctor Hendrick's words. Skyler and I rarely have any interaction on campus that could be considered flirting.

Unless someone knows about one of those private sessions we had in my office.

Or the stairwell.

Or happened to see us that night I dragged her from that club, her body clinging to mine, and her lips pressed to my neck.

Fuck. We weren't being safe at all.

And yet here I am, standing in front of Skyler's table, her warm brown eyes staring up at me like I've hung the moon. "Doctor Reed."

I hear a giggle from somewhere in my periphery, no doubt belonging to Peyton, but all I can see is my gorgeous girl—*naked*. "Miss Mitchell." I nod at her before giving Peyton a warm smile. "Miss White."

"Boston Hottie." She nods politely and I can't escape the chuckle that leaves my lips at her nickname.

"Miss Mitchell, I apologize for the interruption earlier. Did you still have some questions about your paper?"

She grins before screwing the cap back on her water bottle. "I do, actually. Maybe we should go to my apartment and go over them? I'd really like the chance to improve my grade."

I raise an eyebrow at her before looking at Peyton who's staring at us with a devilish smirk. "Go! I own you tonight or tomorrow, Mitchell. It's Halloweekend!" I frown slightly in response to her words.

I suppose walking Skyler to her car is probably not the

best idea, but I'm curious what Peyton meant by *owning* my girlfriend tonight. I'm guessing I won't be spending the night inside her like I hoped?

It's Halloween, dick. She wants to go out and have fun with her friends. See, this is why thirty year old's shouldn't date college students. You're in completely different phases of life.

I try to ignore the annoying thoughts. We pass building after building as we make our way off campus. I look down, staring at the leaves littering the ground that let us know fall is in full swing. "Are you walking me to my car?" Her finger brushes against mine and for a minute my heart lurches in my chest wondering if she's going to slip her hand inside.

"Yes," I tell her. I'm still facing forward and I slide my sunglasses on trying to *look* as professional as possible.

"You sure that's a good idea?"

"I parked in the same lot." A wide smile finds her lips and it almost makes me forget that I have questions about her plans for later. "You're going out with Peyton, I assume?"

"Oh. Yes. Well, I was thinking about it." She fidgets with her hands before looking up at me. "Are you mad about that?"

"Why would I be mad? You're young and in college. You should be going out and enjoying yourself."

"I wish I could enjoy myself *with* you."

"Well, that's not in the cards for us right now. Doctor Hendricks wanted to make sure that I'm keeping everything professional with my students."

"Ah," she says. "What did you say?" She's not looking at me either, allowing me a glimpse of her profile when I cock my head towards her. My eyes trail over her slim neck adorned with a gold chain and infinity charm that she never takes off, even when she sleeps or showers. They trail up to her plump lips that are in a perpetual pout and accentuated on the days she wears red lipstick. *Like today.* Then to her perfectly sculpted nose, and those expressive eyes that control every feeling I have, emphasized by long eyelashes. She turns to look at me and I snap out of my trance.

"What do you think? That I'm sleeping with my student and I have no intentions of stopping? That I spend half my class willing my dick down and not picturing her on her knees in front of me?"

She giggles and there's a slight pep in her step. "Is that foreshadowing? My mouth on your dick?"

I shoot her a salacious grin. "What do you think?

Twenty minutes and three circles around her building later—so that we don't show up at the *exact* same time—I'm walking through Skyler's door to the sound of running water. I don't think twice before shedding my clothes and joining her, my dick leading me through her apartment. We've showered together more times than we've showered apart at my place, but we've never christened her bathroom. I open the door and the steam and smell of her coconut shampoo surrounds me the second I step inside. "Sky?"

"I'll be out in one sec! I just wanted to shower." She peeks her head out and must not notice that I'm naked and moving towards her. I push the curtains back causing her to jump. "Aidan!" she squeals, and I smile as I notice the razor in her hand. "Can you let me shower in peace?" She reaches for the curtain, and I ignore her by stepping into the shower.

"No. Let me help."

"There's not enough room for you in here!" She pushes me slightly but I hold my ground. She furrows her brow at me as I reach for the pink razor in her hand and pulls it back. "Nuh uh. Go away. You're not about to kink up my shower. I literally just wanted to shave and wash my hair."

"What are you shaving?" I look down her body, wondering if I've already missed the part of the show I want to see.

She huffs, though I know she's not going to put up much of a fight. *Skyler loves my kink.* "My legs, do you mind?"

"Not at all, continue."

"You want to watch me shave my legs?"

"That's not all I want to watch." I grin and raise my eyebrows hoping she'll get the message. "Can I help?"

She swallows and looks down at her legs, then back up at me. "You want to shave my legs?"

I see her resolve weakening so I grab the razor from her before she could change her mind about letting her professor shave her legs. I'm on my knees in front of her before she can protest, rubbing her shea butter shaving cream into her right leg. I glide the razor up her leg and over her knee, applying just the right amount of pressure to collect the stray hairs without nicking her. I tighten my grip on the back of her thigh, my fingers rubbing the area where her thigh meets the delicious curve of her ass. I look up to find her lips trapped between her teeth as she looks down at me. "I—I thought I was supposed to be on my knees in front of you," she says.

"Slight change of plans."

I repeat the same with the other leg before rinsing the cream and trailing kisses over the smooth skin. "You have the sexiest legs, Skyler. *Fuck.*" I growl as I bare my teeth and graze her kneecap.

I move my lips up her legs suckling the skin of her inner thigh and she lifts her leg slightly knowing what I want and also telling me what *she* wants. Her leg slides over my shoulder opening her completely up to me, and I want to dive face first into her wet cunt that I know has nothing to do with the water from the shower. I spread the lips of her sex, rubbing my fingers over them.

"Just checking to see if my assistance is needed *here* as well."

Her breath hitches and although the water is still hot, I have a feeling that the reddening of her cheeks has nothing to do with the temperature. I see a few hairs that have grown in, outside of that sexy landing strip she has. "I'm going to eat your pussy till you scream." I tug on a patch of her pubic hair gently. "This is so fucking sexy. I had no idea how much it turned me on until you." I run the blade gently on both sides and the top of her mound before placing it on the side of the tub. My hands wrap around her slim waist, gripping her ass hard as I spear her opening with my tongue.

"Ah!" she cries out as I flick my tongue against her clit. I look up to see her head thrown back against the tile, her eyes squeezed together. "Oh God, Aidan!" She moves her hips in time with my mouth letting me know she's already close. Goosebumps appear on her skin and I can feel her foot flexing against my back. Her sex quivers around me before clenching and I know that means her orgasm is about to hit her, *now.*

She screams out her orgasm, calling my name and God, or maybe she was calling *me* God. But when she finishes she pulls me to stand. "Aidan." She grabs a hold of my dick and pumps it a few times. *"Il tuo corpo è caldo." Your body is hot,* she says and my cock twitches hearing her speak Italian while her hands are on it. I tower over her, my dick tapping the area just above her belly button and she leans down to press a kiss to the head. "Let's get out and go to my bed." She turns off the water and for a moment I'm enthralled as the water droplets continue to rain down her luscious body. All I want to do is catch them with my tongue.

She steps out of the shower, wrapping a towel around her body and her head before darting out of the bathroom towards a closet I know isn't far. She hands me a towel and for a second we're in natural silence. Both of us toweling off like we've been doing this together forever. I watch in fascination as she rubs her lotion into her skin, the smell overwhelming the tiny space of her bathroom and making me dizzy. It's all too much. Her scent coupled with the lotion is creating an aphrodisiac I can't ignore.

"Skyler." My voice is strained as I watch her rub lotion into her perky breasts. I stand up and pull her naked body into my arms, before carrying her from the bathroom. My lips attack hers and our tongues weave between us. Her legs wrap around my waist, and in this moment, I can feel the air shifting around us.

"Voglio fare l'amore con te."

I want to make love to you.

Skyler

I'D NEVER BELIEVED IN LOVE AT FIRST SIGHT. I BELIEVED IT WAS A fallacy constructed by people that wanted to fuck on the first date. Sure, lust at first sight, but love? I may be Italian, which means I have to subscribe to certain romantic beliefs, but love at first sight surely isn't one of them.

And then I met Aidan Reed.

I've come to the startling realization, as I watch him move around my kitchen making me pancakes, that I am in love with him.

That I have *been* in love with him.

Perhaps since I first laid eyes on him. Watching him take those few steps towards me, his eyes fixed on me like he knew every inch of my heart.

"You're staring."

I'm pulled from my thoughts to find Aidan looking at me with a smug grin on his face. "You're cooking me breakfast..." I trail off. *"Shirtless."* The visual stimulation is almost too much and just when I think my panties can't get any wetter, he winks at me.

My phone beeps, effectively snapping me out of my

swooning and I can already imagine who it is and what she's demanding.

Peyton: Brunch. My place. Day drinking commences in one hour. Get your ass out of bed and come over. Doctor big dick can miss you for one day!

I snort at her words, and Aidan turns toward me. "What's so funny?"

"Peyton is summoning me for a day of debauchery."

His jaw tenses and I wonder if he's about to shut down on me. I get off my stool and make my way to him. I wrap my arms around his middle and press my face to his chest. "I wish you could come."

His body is rigid, the hard planes of his chest and torso hard against my face. I pucker my lips and drag them over his heart. I feel his face in my hair. "You'll be careful?"

"I'll just be at Peyton's."

"And then?" he presses.

"I'm not sure." I pull back, wondering where he's going with this. "You know it doesn't matter though, right? I'm yours. I'm not..." I start to say that I'm not like his bitch of an ex-fiancée that broke his heart and had been unfaithful on more than one occasion. "I would never..." I trail off, struggling to find the words. He sighs and hands me the plate with a short stack of what could possibly be the fluffiest pancakes I've ever seen. I set them on the counter and reach my hands up to cup his face. "Aidan, look at me."

"Sky, this is just my shit. I just hate that other guys—other people can spend time with you more freely than I can."

I understand his feelings completely. I feel the same way, that I can't kiss him in broad daylight or even go out on a date with him. I rub my hand harder against his chest, knowing that my hands on him has calmed him the few times he's been agitated around me. "But the semester is half over and then I won't be your student anymore." A part of me wonders if being his student has become part of the allure of our relationship. The forbidden fruit that Aidan tasted and slowly became addicted to. But the look on his face upon hearing my words has me convinced that he is ready for the days that I'm no longer on his student roster.

That day can't come soon enough.

I struggle to keep my eyes open the following Monday morning as the events of the weekend are still fresh in my mind. After going out with Peyton on Saturday, I stumbled home to find a certain professor in my bed, *waiting*. I could barely keep my eyes open, the tequila shots and the several beers I'd bonged at Peyton's postgame hitting me hard. My fatigue was long forgotten the second I'd felt his piercing eyes on me. He had bolted off the bed and pinned me to the wall. I think the sun had just been peeking up over the horizon when he'd let my tired body drift off to sleep in his arms, after hours of the most intense lovemaking I'd ever experienced.

He didn't tell me he loved me but I could feel it with every thrust, every fleeting look, every kiss that made me feel things through every extremity. Aidan loved me and I loved him.

And I'm ready to tell him. Now.

I spent Sunday in the library, away from Aidan and his sinful mouth, knowing that I needed to study, and I couldn't afford the distraction of knowing exactly what that mouth could do.

So now, in his class, a smile crosses my face every time his eyes find mine. He's normally much better about keeping his eyes off me, but today he's let his gaze linger on me more than a few times. When he announces the end of class I take my time putting my stuff away knowing that I have to wait out his fan club to get a moment with him. I frown when I see him bolt from the room. I grab my phone, wanting to inquire why he's left so quickly, when there's a message waiting for me.

Aidan: My office. Don't make me tell you twice.

My eyes dart around the room, as if people could see the message on my phone. I wonder if they can hear the loud pounding in my chest or can tell that my breathing has accelerated. I get up quickly and slide my MacBook Pro into my bag before letting my hormones lead me to his office, all the while ignoring my pesky subconscious whispering, *this is a bad idea, Skyler.*

I push through his office door and his eyes must have been trained on it because he's staring at me. He's out of his chair in an instant moving around the room and unbuckling his pants. "Fucking hell, Skyler, you bit your lip for a full hour," he growls. He reaches for me, pulling me into my arms and pressing his face into my neck as he inhales my scent. *"Dammi un bacio."* Give me a kiss.

I pull away and present my lips to him which he takes greedily. He bites down on my bottom lip before licking the sting away with his tongue and sliding it into my mouth. He lifts me in his arms and pins me to the door, pressing his cock against me. It's one of those rare warm November days and I'm grateful for the temperature that persuaded me to wear a skirt this morning which allows me to feel him *closely.* "Aidan," I moan as I hear his slacks hit the ground and the only things separating us are thin layers of underwear.

"Slide your panties to the side. Let me in, baby." I don't know when exactly we'd stopped using condoms altogether. For a while, Aidan suggested that we use them intermittently just so he wasn't coming inside of me every time. *Especially with the frequency in which we had sex.*

I do as he asks and he slips in, burying his cock deep inside of me. The lips of my sex kiss the base of his cock as he stretches me to accommodate his thick member. I'm used to his size but it doesn't stop me from feeling the delicious pierce whenever he slides in and the ache that follows when he leaves the space between my legs. My legs wrap around his waist as he thrusts inside, each stroke harder than the one before. I can tell he's already close by the way he's fucking me, making me wonder if my lip biting had really done a number on him. "Do you need me to come?" I whisper against his neck. I know the answer before he responds.

"More than my next fucking breath." His lips drag along my neck, and his fingers dig into my hips with every thrust. I know he's trying to wait for me before he explodes. "You know I need your sexy moans. The way your cunt squeezes me when you orgasm. The way your face twists in pleasure and you whimper out my name. I need your juices slipping out of you and dripping down my dick."

His words are my undoing and the orgasm hits me out of nowhere. "Oh my God, Aidan!" I scream into his jacket, the fabric muffling my words as he grunts out his climax. I feel his dick pulsing inside me as I imagine jets of cum shooting out of him and into me. For a second, the thought of that cum producing life inside of me sparks and blooms in my chest.

I let out a breath as I try and break the sex haze that has me thinking these crazy thoughts.

"Fuck. Skyler, baby." He rubs his nose against mine and when my eyes flutter open, his are staring into mine. He's still inside of me, though he's softened dramatically, and I swallow, wondering if he's about to say the three words I've been dying to say. "You mean so much to me, you know that?" I nod, the force of my orgasm and the intensity of the moment rendering me speechless. *"Potrei guardarti tutto il giorno,"* he whispers against my lips. *I could look at you all day.* He pulls out of me slowly and I wince at the loss of contact, and the emptiness I feel has my eyes welling up with tears. I sniffle, drawing his attention back to me after he's grabbed some tissues from his desk. "What is it, baby? Did I do something?"

"No!" I say quickly. "You're perfect. This is just...intense. I never thought I would feel like this." I let out a breath. "I've never felt like this." Aidan's eyes trace my face and I wonder if he can see what I'm trying to say. He's privy to my relationship with Gabriel, and he knows that at the time I believed that I was in love. I wonder if he's pieced it together that I'm in love with him.

"Me neither," he murmurs and a gasp escapes my lips. *He's been in love once.*

For him to say that means he loves me.

My eyes plead with him to speak the words. *Say it, Aidan. Let me know this is real.*

We stare at each other for I don't know how long when his phone beeps, breaking us from the moment. My eyes dart to the phone on his desk and I nod at it. He backs up, keeping his eyes on me before he breaks the connection to look at the screen. "Dammit." He sighs.

"What?"

"Hendricks wants to see me in his office. I swear that old man is a pain in the ass."

I giggle and smooth my skirt down. "I should be going anyway. I have an English paper due at the end of the week."

"What's it on, want my help?"

I shake my head. "As helpful as you may be on *Romeo and Juliet*, I think I have it under control." I laugh and he frowns.

"We aren't a tragedy, Sky."

"That's not what I meant, only the part about not being able to be together, that's all."

He nods before tucking a hair behind my ear. "I'll see you later, tonight?"

"You'll come over?" I ask, the excitement in my voice at seeing him later overtaking me.

"Nothing could keep me away." He presses his lips to mine so gently and sweetly I almost combust. My knees weaken and he catches me, wrapping his arm around my back to keep me upright.

My eyes flutter open long after his lips leave mine, the skin still tingling. "I'll see you later."

We make our way out of his office and begin towards the main entrance when I spot Doctor Hendricks walking towards us. "Fuck," I hear him grumble.

"Doctor Reed, I was on my way to your office. I wasn't sure if you saw my email."

"I saw it. I was in the middle of office hours," Aidan says without missing a beat.

"Odd. I thought your hours were from four to six?" The accusation isn't blatant but I can hear it and I try to appear like my heart isn't racing.

"Oh, I wasn't able to make his hours today, and I asked if he could meet after class," I speak up. Both men look at me and Doctor Hendricks sizes me up the way a father looks at his daughter right before he tells her to go upstairs and change before she can step foot outside the house. The floral scarf wrapped around my neck hides my cleavage but my legs are on display. I'll admit my skirt is a little short, as I do dress to kill on the days I have Aidan's class.

Doctor Hendricks nods at me. "I see. And what's your name, Miss?"

"Skyler Mitchell, sir. I'm a freshman."

"Ah. Miss Mitchell. Yes, I'm familiar. Your father, Preston Mitchell?"

"One and the same."

"Well, we are pleased to have you as a part of the Criminal Justice Department." He gives me a look before turning to Aidan and then back to me. This is the second time he's seen us together and the way he's looking at us, it's a thought not lost on him. *Fuck.*

"Thank you." I nod politely before turning to Aidan. "Thank you again for your help, Doctor Reed." I turn and walk away, all the while thinking that maybe the love story of Aidan and I will be a tragedy after all.

There's a crowd around Peyton's usual table when I approach it and she immediately shoos one of the guys away. "Make room for Skyler." Her sleek blonde strands are pushed back by a headband that matches a tweed mini dress over a blouse. She looks like a modern day Cher from *Clueless,* and I swear only she could make it work. I sit next to her as everyone continues to talk. "So, you coming?" I hear from my other side and I turn to see a guy with some Greek letters scattered across his t-shirt and a smile, which is probably a lethal combination for most girls.

"Sorry? Coming where?"

"To our party this weekend. Homecoming weekend is always huge. I hate that it's so late this year but should still be pretty lit." He smiles, revealing two deep dimples underneath a smattering of stubble and a perfect grin. "I'm Dave."

"Skyler." I give him a small smile because even though I have a boyfriend, and I have enough awareness to know that this guy is definitely trying to flirt with me, I'm polite.

"I know. Peyton's cute Italian friend." He winks.

I roll my eyes at my claim to fame. "Is that my tagline?"

"No, but Peyton doesn't have many girl friends."

I turn to look at her as she commands the table of men like they're her loyal subjects. I'm just about to answer when the air shifts around me. My thighs push together on their own accord, a shiver snakes down my spine even though there isn't a breeze and my throat suddenly becomes dry.

I feel him before I even see him. I crane my neck to look behind me and I see Aidan sitting a table over his eyes trained on me despite the sunglasses over his eyes. I swallow and my eyes dart around the quad looking for anyone that may be paying attention to the potential interaction. "Dave, I actually left something in my last class. Sorry." I start to stand and he stands with me.

"I could walk with you? I have to hit the library anyway." And for a moment, I wonder what would have happened if I had never met Aidan. *Could I let this cute frat boy court me? Date me? Letter me? Maybe even lavalier me if I made the decision to join a sorority?* I realize none of that matters because I did meet Aidan and I do belong to him, even if we can't go out on dates or tailgates or study together in the library. He's mine and I'm his, even with all the obstacles in the way.

"Thank you, but…I'm okay…" I start to say I have a boyfriend but frankly, I'm not ready for the questions I'd have to lie to answer: most importantly, *who?* I'm off the bench before he can respond and rushing towards the nearest building, praying that Aidan will follow me. I don't make it two steps down a hallway before I'm hauled into an empty classroom and he closes the door behind him.

"Hi," I whisper, my teeth finding my bottom lip instantly.

He crosses his arms over his chest and I can sense the tension flowing off him in waves. "That guy wants you."

"Does it matter?"

"Did he ask you out?"

"No," I tell him. "He just asked if I was coming to a party this weekend." I hurry to add, "I won't go if you don't want me to." Aidan's not looking at me, his gaze trained on the floor as he struggles to meet my eyes.

"Doesn't matter," he mumbles and my eyebrows draw together.

"What does that mean?"

"It means I'm never going to be able to have you, Skyler. And I can't keep asking you to give up college experiences for me. When I was nineteen, I wouldn't have given them up for anything."

"Why—why can't you have me? I'm only your student for another six weeks. Just until winter break."

"Try until May 2022," he says and I stare at him confused. "Hendricks informed me, after he made note that I needed to stay away from *you*, Skyler, that teachers are prohibited to be in a relationship with *any* student on campus—mine or otherwise."

"What? That's absurd."

"No students, no teachers. Period. Ever. They said it keeps all bases covered."

"So…"

"So, you're off limits to me for four years."

His words are like a punch in the stomach, leaving me gasping for air. I open my mouth to take in a deep breath and look around the abandoned classroom to try and collect my thoughts. "What did he say about me?" I ask weakly.

"He said that he's seen me alone with you more than once now and asked point blank if anything was going on. I said no and he advised I keep it that way, especially with you being the chancellor's niece."

"Goddaughter," I correct, though I'm not sure why. Maybe if we aren't blood-related, Aidan will feel less intimidated.

"Whatever," he grumbles. I take a step forward and he holds his hand out stopping me in place. "Skyler…"

"This sucks," I whisper, "but I don't want to give you up. Give *us* up." He's silent and my heart begins to accelerate wondering what it means. "I can quit after this semester. I can transfer to—"

"No." His word is strong like there's no room for explanation or rebuttal.

"But, Aidan…"

"No Skyler, absolutely not."

"But…" I don't even try to stop the tears from flowing down my face. "But I love you." My words cause a knee-jerk reaction. He presses off the door instantly and frames my face with his hands. He doesn't say anything, he just searches my face with those blue eyes. *Reading me. Seeing me.* "Don't…I mean, do you feel the same?" I'm not sure what prompted me to ask, but I have to know.

He closes his eyes and rests his forehead against mine. "If I tell you I feel the same, that makes this so much harder." His words aren't *I love you*, but I hear the sentiment, and a part of me wishes he would have just said he didn't love me. To be honest, I think that would hurt less.

I choke back a sob before pulling away. "I'm supposed to stay away from you for four years? And then what? We be together? Let's say I could hold out 'till then, would you even wait for me? I can't expect you to not date other women between now and then. You're gorgeous. Women throw themselves at you."

"*Tu sei l'unica per me.*" *You're the only one for me.*

"Cut the shit, Aidan. That's not what I asked." I stomp my foot, not letting him use Italian to get out of this.

He looks at me, surprised by my outburst. "I belong to you, Skyler."

"Then don't give me up!"

"What other choice do we have? I can't do this for four years. We'll get caught. We were seconds from getting caught earlier. Could you imagine if he knocked while I was nailing you against the door? With the scent of our sex in the air and my dick hanging out of my pants. I'm reckless when it comes to you, Skyler. I can't think, and it's going to ruin everything. My career, *your* future."

I swallow and rub my hand across my tattoo. *La vita va avanti.*

Life goes on.
Life goes on.
Life goes on.

"I'm so stupid," I whisper, the tears falling down my face. "I always do this. Get involved too quickly and intensely. I throw myself into things without thinking of the repercussions and then I get hurt because I do things with my whole heart." My lip trembles and I don't know if I'm angrier at myself for getting into this mess or Aidan for not stopping things before they got this far.

"Baby, you're not stupid." He wraps his arms around me and, despite the fact that I know this is the end, I let him hold me while I begin to mourn Aidan and Skyler. A love that burned fast and bright before exploding into stars that faded into darkness.

A shooting star.

"I don't want this to end." I make one final plea, hoping that I can convince him that we are worth the risk. "Please."

"Il mio cuore batte solo per te." My heart only beats for you, he whispers into my hair. His voice is quiet, but my sobs have slowed and I hear him clear as day.

"Tell me you love me." I look up at him and the face he gives me breaks my heart.

"If I say that, I'll never let you go."

"But you do…love me."

He swallows and lets out a breath breaking the connection between us. "I should go."

"Aidan." I take a step towards him as he takes a step back.

"I'm trying to do the right thing. Let me."

"By breaking my heart? How is that the right thing?"

"One day you'll thank me, I promise, Skyler."

"No! Don't you dare make this about teaching me some lesson I'll understand down the road. Like I'm too naive to understand now. Love knows no age, Aidan. I love you and I know you love me too. We can get through this…*together*. We will make it work!" I hate myself for sounding so pitiful. My voice so desperate and pleading as I try my best to keep my heart from breaking. *Maybe I really am too young.*

"I'm sorry, Skyler, I just…*can't.*" I hear his words but his body language doesn't match. His posture is tense and rigid, his breathing labored, and his eyes give him away. Piercing blue eyes that used to heat me with a glance are dull, lifeless and empty. The hurt behind them is so evident. Tortured orbs that crush me because the pain in them is a direct reflection of mine.

He stands at the door, his hand resting on the door handle as he stares at me. He starts to speak before he shakes his head, and then he's gone making me wish I'd never come to CGU.

That I'd never joined that stupid dating app.

That I hadn't chosen criminal justice because that's what my dad wanted.

That I hadn't put my heart out there again.

My heart thumps in my chest in protest.

I don't regret one second of my time with Aidan.

But it doesn't make it hurt any less.

Aidan

THE DRIVE HOME TO MY APARTMENT IS A BLUR; MY MIND barely focuses on the road as buildings and trees pass me. Traffic in DC at this hour has become the bane of my existence and I'm shocked I don't rear end anyone with my mind completely focused on Skyler, remembering that look in her eyes when I left her in that classroom.

Dick move. You should have at least walked her to her car.

But I couldn't.

I knew if I stayed in that room a second longer, if I stared into her warm brown eyes for another beat I'd confess every thought I'd had about her over the past month. But most importantly the three words that had been roaring in my head for the past week. The words were almost suffocating, they tried to claw their way out of my chest making it difficult to breathe in the confines of that classroom.

I love you.

I squeeze my eyes shut as I slam the door to my apartment behind me so hard that the picture on my wall rattles under the force. I stare at the abstract painting my sister said I "had to have" because I'm over thirty and my mural of vinyl records is "so late twenties." I'm not even sure what I'm looking at, but all I see is Skyler. The browns in the painting are almost the exact color of her eyes and I know they would be all I see in my dreams later.

I march to the refrigerator and pull out a beer, downing it in one gulp before realizing that I will definitely need something stronger to get through the night.

I'm sorry, Skyler. Forgive me, please.

A part of me wonders if I'm a coward for not telling her how I feel. For letting Hendricks get in my head. But then I remember the look in his eyes.

He was serious.

"Sit down, Doctor Reed," he orders as he closes the door to his office. The air is thick and tense and I try my best to keep my cool, but I'm ready to hand this cantankerous old man his ass if he's ready to spout accusations again.

I almost tell him I would prefer standing but I suppose the less combative I am the better. "What's this meeting about?"

"Well, it was about whether you could help out with a panel this weekend for homecoming. Now, it's about something else entirely." He sits down across from me, a polished, rich mahogany desk between us, and a mountain of papers that looked in desperate need of organization. "What is going on with you and Preston Mitchell's daughter?"

I hate the way he addresses her. Like she has no identity outside of being her father's daughter—who I assume to be a large benefactor and prominent alumni. Skyler is so much more than that. She is bright and passionate and has her whole life ahead of her. Her parents don't control her narrative. She doesn't have to live in the shadow of her father.

"I'm not sure what you mean. Skyler Mitchell is a student. Nothing more."

He leans back in his chair and stares at me, steepling his fingers under his chin. "Aidan," he says. "You know I've been doing this a long time. Going on almost thirty years. You can't pull the wool over my eyes."

"I'm not doing anything. She's a student and frankly, these accusations are getting old. And a little out of line. Take me to HR if you're so concerned." I go to stand when he stops me.

"Skyler Mitchell is off limits, Doctor Reed. You need to stay away from her."

"I already said—" I start when he interrupts me.

"I know what you said. But I've seen you alone with her on more than one occasion now. Have you been…" He clears his throat. "I'm just going to ask point blank. Are you sleeping with her?"

I know I don't have but a second to respond, but it's enough time to hate myself for denying my feelings for Skyler or the fact that what I do with my woman doesn't concern anyone on this god damn campus. She doesn't belong to CGU or her father or this department.

She belongs to me.

"No, Doctor Hendricks, and frankly, you're out of line. You've seen me twice with a student ON campus, and suddenly I'm sleeping with her. I'm not going to stand for this kind of harassment just because my students actually enjoy my class." I shoot him a look implying that students don't quite feel the same about his class.

"A simple no would have sufficed. No need to get defensive and… offensive." He pushes his glasses up on the bridge of his nose.

"Is that all? I have things to do that don't involve being interrogated for building relationships with my students."

"I'll email you about the panel," he says as he turns to his computer.

"I never agreed to—" I start.

He doesn't look up from his computer before he interrupts me. "I'll email you about the panel."

I turn to leave when I hear his voice again, "Doctor Reed."

I turn around slowly. "Yes, Doctor Hendricks?"

He sighs and rubs a hand over his jaw. "Maybe you haven't done anything yet, so in case you were thinking that all you have to do is get through this semester..." he trails off. "Teachers are prohibited from being in a relationship with any student at any time during their tenure. That means sophomores, juniors, and seniors are off limits as well. It's not just your students." He turns back to his computer, thankfully, because the look on my face can't be controlled.

What? What kind of bullshit rule is that? I always thought that as long as the person in question wasn't your actual student it might be frowned upon but wasn't prohibited.

I realize I haven't moved. I'm frozen in place, and he looks up at me with a knowing look. "Things get messy and the school just prefers a clean line. Black. White. No gray."

"But that's not how life works...the world is full of gray." I hadn't expected to argue but it tumbles out of my mouth before I can stop it.

"It's how life works at CGU, Doctor Reed."

🌹

I stare at one of the many pictures I have of her on my phone. She's lying on her side in my bed, wearing my t-shirt. Her eyes are closed and she has a sleepy smile on her face. I snapped the photo and a moment later she was in my arms attacking my face with her lips. I'm just about to toss my phone to the side to avoid staring at her beautiful face a second longer when it comes to life in my hands. Even as I see the name flash across the screen I pray it reads something different. Had it been anyone else, I would have ignored it. With the exception of a short, pretty Italian girl that has taken up residence in my heart, this is the only person whose phone call I would take.

"Hey, Ma." I try my best to sound like I'm not as depressed as I feel.

"My favorite son!" I can hear the smile in her voice and I know without even seeing her that she's standing in the kitchen twirling the cord of the phone around her hand because *"I have a house phone, why do I need to use my cellphone in the house? And also texting is for when you don't want to hear someone's voice. I always want to hear my babies' voices."*

"I'm your only son," I laugh. "But I know I'm also your favorite child." I'm the oldest of three, with two younger sisters that drove my parents, and more importantly my mother, completely nuts. I, on the other hand, am the golden child that never gave them any issues.

"Oh, don't say that. You know that upsets the girls."

"Only because they know it's true. What's up, Ma?"

"I was just calling to see how you like D.C.? Is everyone nice? Is the traffic as bad as they say? Have you gone to the monuments? Have you seen Obama? I saw on the Twitter that he likes this particular ice cream shop and this restaurant on 14th Street."

I laugh thinking about my mother's fascination with the forty-fourth president. "No, unfortunately, I haven't seen him. I have my eyes open though."

"Picture and autograph, Aiden. You promised."

"I know. I know." I lean my head back against the chair and let out a sigh that I instantly regret remembering who I'm on the phone with.

The silence is deafening. *Here it comes.* "Talk to me, honey. What's wrong?"

"Nothing. I'm just tired."

"Try again. I know when something's bothering you. And I know when it's anything but fatigue. I saw you through four years of high school sports." I'm silent and she speaks again. "Is it a girl?"

I'm instantly irritated that she knows me so well, but I have a sneaking suspicion that Chace probably told James who told my sister who told my mother that I had met someone. Or maybe it was mother's intuition.

"Mom..." I trail off. "I really don't want to talk about it."

"Too bad. Speak. That stupid Corinne better not have contacted you."

"No, Ma. I just..."

"Do you love her?" The word is on the tip of my tongue but I can't make myself say it.

"I haven't told her."

"But you do." I'm silent and she huffs. "Aidan Michael Reed, I don't care how old you are or how many degrees you have, or the fancy suffix in front of your name. I will still ground the hell out of you for lying to me."

"Oh really?" I chuckle as I grab another beer and take a large gulp.

"Does she love you?"

"Yes."

"Then what's the problem?"

"What do you think the problem is?" My mother was smart and could read situations instantly.

"I don't know. Intimacy issues?" The beer flies from my mouth and spews all over my coffee table.

"Ma!" I manage to yell between coughs.

"What? I don't know, Aidan. Tell me."

"She's a student," I sigh.

"*Whose* student?" she asks, but I can hear the tone in her voice. *I think I know what you're trying to say, but I'll give you a chance to correct me for my assumption. Correct me, Aidan Michael.*

"*My* student."

"Jesus, Mary, and Joseph, Aidan. Is she even legal?"

"Yes, Mother!"

"Aren't you teaching first year students?"

"She's nineteen," I grit out.

"And you're how old? You know what, don't answer that, I don't need the reminder of how old *I* am." I roll my eyes as I think about celebrating my mother's forty-fifth birthday for the umpteenth time. *She and I are going to be the same age here soon.* "Sweetheart, I would never judge you. But isn't that usually…frowned upon?"

"Now you understand the reason for my sigh, don't you?"

"Watch your tone, Aidan."

I swallow the lump in my throat, preparing myself to say the words aloud. "I love her."

"What's the problem then?"

"The whole her being my student thing?"

"Well, can't you just hide it until she's no longer your student?"

"No, Mother, I hadn't thought of that." My voice is laced with sarcasm. "Teachers are prohibited from relationships with any students at all. So, I can't be with her until she graduates four years from now. And the dean of our college is already onto us. I can't hide our relationship for four years, Ma. I wear my feelings for her all over my face."

"Oh, honey."

"She said she'd quit…but I can't let her do that. She'd regret it and then she would eventually resent me."

"More than she'd regret not being with someone she loves?"

"She's young. And she thought she was in love once before. Who knows if she really loves me."

"Don't use her age as a reason to push her away. I've been in love with your father since I was seventeen."

My heart constricts hearing her words. I know that's part of the reason why I may have unrealistic expectations about love. My parents have been in love since they were teenagers and even now, thirty-five years later, they are still wild about each other.

"You're the exception, not the rule."

"*You* are exceptional, Aidan."

I smile, hearing her words. Maryanne Reed always knew just what to say when I felt like shit. *Skyler would love her.* "Thanks, Ma."

"Now tell me about her, Son."

I should have stopped after the third whiskey.

Definitely after the fourth.

I curse myself for the fifth when I'm in front of Skyler's door pounding on it at two in the morning. "Baby, open the door, please." I'm leaning against the door, knocking every few seconds when it opens and I almost fall through. I manage to catch my balance and she closes the door behind me.

"What are you doing here?" she asks and I take a second to look at her. She's wearing CGU sweatpants and one of my Harvard faculty t-shirts that I had from my time there. Her face is pale and her eyes are red, like she's been bawling for the past few hours. Her hair is up in a ponytail with several strands falling from the holder, and I notice her lip trembling slightly.

"I needed you to know something." I hiccup and she sighs, letting her eyes close.

"You're drunk."

"No." I hiccup again. *Fuck. Get it together, Aidan.* "Don't make me leave."

I can tell she's at war with herself about whether she should do just that when she walks by me and into her kitchen. I follow closely behind her and almost bump into her when she hands me a bottle of water. "Why are you here?"

"Because I love you. And…I hate that you hate me. That I fucked everything up."

"You didn't fuck anything up. And I certainly don't hate you." She swallows. "But let's circle back to the first thing… you love me?"

"Very much."

Tears swim in her eyes and threaten to move down her cheeks, but she brushes them away. "But it doesn't change anything, does it?"

"I couldn't have you…going on with your life thinking that things weren't real for me too. That I didn't feel…what you felt."

Her breath hitches and then the tears are moving down her face rapidly and I hate myself for putting them there. "Please," she whimpers, "don't."

I wrap my arms around her and press her face to my chest. "Princess, please don't cry."

"I don't want to say goodbye to you. I can't." Her pleas make my heart beat faster and I wish I could do something to take away her pain.

"If I would have known that the last time I touched you was the last time, I never would have let go," I whisper in her ear. "I wouldn't have fucked you against the door. I would have laid you down and worshipped every inch of your body. I would have made love to you until our bodies couldn't go on another second. I would have memorized you."

She looks up at me, her gaze watery and pained. "You can do that now..." she whispers and my cock springs to life, screaming at my body to sober up.

"Skyler..." I trail off.

She nods her head once and backs up out of my arms. "I get that we can't be together, but maybe...one more time?" She puts one finger up, bites down on her bottom lip, and I *lose* it. I crush my lips to hers, groaning into her perfect mouth before lifting her into my arms. I'm kissing her like it's the last time and I pour everything into it. She's kissing me back with equal fervor and I melt into her lips, carrying her to her couch and sitting her in my lap.

"My bedroom..." She points to the room that I've spent just as much time in as she has since she moved in, and I nod.

"I know. We'll get there. I'm not in a rush. Unless...you want to go back to bed?"

"I wasn't sleeping," she mumbles. "I couldn't sleep. And I would give up all of my sleep for one last night with you."

"You know why I'm doing this, right? I hate that I'm hurting you."

"I understand." She looks down at where she's sitting on top of me and I can't wait until I can feel her skin to skin. "I don't like it though."

"Bella..." I trail kisses down her neck and she raises her arms allowing me to pull my t-shirt over her head.

"Can I keep that?" Her eyes find the shirt on the ground.

"I'm keeping all the underwear I've stolen," I tell her, jokingly, though I'm one hundred percent serious.

She furrows her brow and looks at me. "Please don't joke."

"I'm sorry, princess." I look at her naked chest, and run my fingers over her nipples, tweaking them between my fingers. "So perfect."

"Hai cambiato la mia vita, Aidan," she whispers. *You changed my life.* "It'll go on, but it'll be different." She plays with the buttons on my shirt, undoing them slowly one by one and kissing every inch of skin that's exposed beneath it. "I love you," she whispers before she nuzzles my neck. She stands up out of my arms and slides her sweatpants and underwear down her legs before tossing them to the side, leaving her completely naked in front of me. My mouth waters and I palm my cock, willing the ache away so I don't explode before I'm inside of her. I unbutton my slacks and pull them off along with my briefs and begin to stroke my cock at the sight of her. She moves back to my lap and smacks my hand away before she slides down on me with nothing between us. "Fuck," she whispers.

"Ti amo," I whisper in her ear as she slides down. *I love you.* She cries out in response, more than likely due to me filling her completely, but I think my words helped.

"Oh God!" she screams as she slams down on me again. She's bouncing on me faster and I attach my lips to her right nipple before her left, savoring the taste of her sweet skin. I am going to miss the taste of her nipples, vanilla from her body butter and her natural essences. I tug one between my teeth and bite down gently before I let her go with a pop.

"Promise me you'll enjoy your college years, baby. That you'll stay safe but you'll enjoy your life."

"I'll t-try," she stammers and I'm not sure if it's because she's turned on or upset or maybe a combination of both.

"Promise me." I grab her jaw and make our eyes lock.

"My Bella," I whisper as I hold up her arm and rub my lips across her tattoo. *"La vita va avanti*, right?"

I'm still inside her but she's stopped moving. "Yes." She nods before she begins to move up and down again. Her eyes are wide and unblinking, staring into mine as we move towards our release. "Tell me this isn't the end. That we'll find our way back to each other when this is all over. Please, Aidan."

"Baby..." *I want nothing more than to promise her that. That I will wait until she graduates. That I will watch from the sidelines as she grows into the woman she's supposed to be. But I can't. I can't let her potential future with me control her destiny. She would always have me in the back of her mind and it may influence her decisions. She could turn down opportunities that would take her elsewhere because she'd be trying to preserve our future together. I may be ready to get married and start a family but I know she isn't. So, I have to let her go.*

She has her whole life ahead of her and it's just beginning. I can't tie her down just when she's about to spread her wings and take flight.

One day she'd look back and wish she hadn't traded everything for a hidden romance with me.

I stare into her eyes and even as I think the words I don't know if I believe them.

She'd want to take these adventures with you.

"I never say never," I say before I press my lips to hers hoping that would suffice.

I trail kisses down her cheek and neck and she sighs after being effectively fucked to sleep. She snuggles closer to me, her hands gripping me even in slumber. Her lips are parted and I trail my index finger over her bottom lip. I grip her jaw and place a kiss on her lips. We had been at it for hours before she fell asleep in my arms, the tears leaking from her eyes. The sun is rising and slowly peeking through her blinds, illuminating the room, and while I want to call in sick for my classes today, I know I can't.

I have to move on, or try to move on. I press my lips to hers and move on top of her, hovering above her to sink into her one final time. I burrow my nose in her hair, trying to ingrain her scent into my memory. Her pussy is still slick with arousal after I had just been inside her no more than an hour ago.

"Wake up, sweetheart." Her eyes fly open, like she wasn't deep asleep yet, and her legs wrap around my waist. "I have to go." I drop my head into the crook of her neck and lick the skin.

"I know." Her voice breaks and I try to make her feel better by thrusting harder.

"But come for me first. You better fucking come all over my cock. Remember how good it feels. Me inside of you. Remember how hard you come, how alive you feel when I'm inside of you. Never forget this, baby."

"Never," she whimpers. "Don't *you* forget *me*." Her pussy is quivering around me and I know she's close. I almost pull out of her so that we can start the climb towards her climax all over. *I never want this moment to end.*

"Come for me, Sky. I need to feel you." I pluck her nipples, feeling the pebbled skin under my hand.

"Aidan!"

Her cry makes my balls jump up, preparing to release my seed inside of her. And then she screams. She screams so loud

I can feel it in every bone in my body. A scream so visceral I can't tell if she's in pleasure or pain.

Probably a little of both.

I wring her petite body of the last of her orgasm and she sighs, feeling content, and what I assume to be thoroughly fucked. I begin to thrust faster and mine comes like a bolt of electricity, sending a shock through my system. I pull out just as I begin to orgasm and she wraps her legs tighter around me. "No stay," she begs.

"I want to see my cum on you," I growl just before I break free of her hold and come all over her flat stomach and the top of her pussy. "I need this memory. You laying out on your bed, thoroughly fucked underneath a layer of...*me.*"

I drag my hand through the orgasm sitting on her stomach and begin to rub it into her skin. "Don't hate me for being so selfish," I tell her and she looks at me oddly. "For needing you one last time."

"Never," she whispers as she clings to me. We don't say anything after that as our breathing returns to normal. We lay side by side, our fingers interlaced when she speaks into the dimly lit room.

"I don't think I can come to class. I won't be able to keep it together."

"I'll give you an A regardless, Skyler. You deserve it. Just come in for the final and turn in your last two papers."

She nods and I turn my face toward her. I watch helplessly as the tears leak from her eyes. "I can't watch you leave." She turns on her side, away from me, and I watch as her shoulders shake up and down. I wrap my arms around her and press my lips to her neck.

"*Ciao, Bella.*" *Goodbye, beautiful.*

Skyler

I MISS AIDAN.

There is no other way to describe the way I'm feeling. I'm in love with a man I can't have and I'm being forced to accept it. It's been three weeks since he left my apartment, taking my heart with him, and I hadn't seen him since. I hadn't been to class, and I think he's avoided the quad like the plague, knowing I usually hang around there with Peyton between classes.

I try my best to put him out of my head while I'm in class, not wanting to destroy the straight A's I'd been maintaining up until now. Despite the pain, I have to focus.

"Everything is going to be fine." Peyton's voice breaks me from my thoughts. "I let you be a recluse all semester. It's time to have some fun." Dave's frat—the guys of Alpha…Pi…Tau…Omega…Epsilon, *whatever they all sound the same*—are having a party tonight and I'd been convinced that *socialization* was needed.

Peyton had gone above and beyond her call of duty, rarely leaving me alone with my thoughts and having crashed at my apartment so I didn't dwell too much in the late hours of the night. She hadn't pushed but she had learned what all my silences meant. She knew when I needed to get my mind off of it, and when I just wanted silence. There were moments when it hurt less, where I was able to get my mind off of it, but that usually involved an SVU marathon and sausage pizza. I'd taken up running as I tried to avoid the ten pounds I'd put on after my last round of "heartbreak." And in those moments, where all I focused on was putting one foot in front of the other, I made myself forget him.

"I know. I appreciate you doing everything you've done for me this semester. You're the best, Peyton." *And I mean that.* Friends like Peyton didn't come along but maybe once or twice in your life and I know she's someone I'll be friends with when CGU is a distant memory.

There were a few nights I let Peyton get me drunk and one or two where I'd gotten high, trying to numb the pain for just a second. The tequila made me sick for the first time in my entire life, and then I spent the night on my bathroom floor sobbing my eyes out. The weed successfully mellowed me out, but it also made me think. *Too much.* And then I ate an entire pizza in the span of forty-five minutes.

The wind whips around us and I pull my leather jacket harder around me. It isn't cold quite yet, but the seasons are changing. With every day that passes, the weather ticks a degree cooler in the evenings and while I've learned that the weather here is fickle, I know winter is coming. I'd curled my hair in soft waves and it flows now in the cool wind behind me. "Don't sweat it, Sky. This is going to be fun. Just maybe no tequila shots for you." Peyton raises an eyebrow as we make it to the house.

There's a guy outside smoking a cigarette with two other guys and he nods at Peyton. "Hey, P. Been a minute, where you been?" He takes a sharpie and puts X's on our hands and she shrugs.

"Around. Been hanging at better frats." She shoots him a cheeky grin in response to his pointed look. "Get out of here, troublemaker. Keg's in the back." He nods at me and gives me a smile. "P's friend."

I offer a wave and a small smile as we enter the house and are instantly met with the sounds of Drake. We push our way through the crowded house to the back patio and a group of guys surrounding the keg. "Peyton! Skyler!" I try to avoid the sinking feeling of seeing Dave, knowing that I'm going to be spending the night warding off his advances. He's harmless, but he just isn't who I want. "I had no idea you guys were coming, I would have gotten you guys house cups."

A house cup, which I'd learned was every girl's dream at a fraternity, meant you didn't have to wait in line for beer. I should have been excited, but it usually meant the guy was getting something in return at the end of the night.

"All good, it was last minute," Peyton says as he pumps our beers for us.

"I've barely seen you the last few weeks, where you been hiding?" He taps her nose and shoots me a grin. *What a flirt.*

"Oh, you know," Peyton says with a flick of her wrist before grabbing her beers. "Let's go dance, Sky."

"I'll be in later. Save me one?" He winks at me and I realize I haven't spoken a word since we walked inside.

"Right, umm, okay," I manage before following Peyton inside.

"You don't have to dance with him," Peyton tells me as she takes a healthy swallow of her beer. "You don't have to do anything you don't want to."

"I know…I just…maybe I should?"

"I support it!" She gives me a thumbs up as she drags me to the center of the circle. "Thanks for letting me drag you out."

"Got to start moving on somehow, right?"

Peyton doesn't say anything. She just stares at me with a look in her eyes that I can't quite detect. *Is it pity?*

"Oh my gosh, Skyler!" I turn my head to see a familiar redhead come into view. She's clearly intoxicated as she throws her arms around me. "It's me, Lily…from Dr. Reed's class?"

My heart constricts hearing his name and I try to clear the tears forming with a cough. "Right, hey!"

"I haven't seen you in ages! Did you drop his class? I haven't seen you!"

"No…I…I've just had a lot going on."

"Damn, you must not need the extra credit points. Lucky bitch! I bombed his last exam. But it helps that he's really nice to look at. So, I don't mind *sooo* much about going to class." She runs a hand through her hair before tucking a wild curl behind her ear. "He's been weird though."

"Weird?" I ask. I know I shouldn't ask. I don't want to hear anything about him. I'd severed all connections with him. I'd even deactivated my Instagram so I wouldn't be tempted to stalk him. This resulted in an immediate call from my sister wondering who the fuck broke my heart now because that was the only time I deleted social media. *Bitch.*

"Yeah, he was like funny and cool before. Now he's just rigid and straightforward. He doesn't even hold office hours anymore. All communication is through email or when he holds a group session the week of a test. Word on the street is some teachers were speculating that girls cared more about *him* than his class. So, I guess he's just trying to keep his job."

"Right…yeah, well. I guess." I'm not sure what to say to that. But I'm happy that he's keeping all females at arm's length.

"Will you be there on Monday? He hinted there would be a pop quiz…" She winced. "Just a heads up." She downs the rest of her drink and wipes her mouth before looking inside her cup like she's surprised it's all gone.

"Oh… umm, maybe then." My mind is all out of sorts hearing about Aidan. Between the booze we'd drank at Peyton's earlier mixed with this revelation, I can't form a coherent thought.

She cranes her eyes towards the keg and begins to walk away. "Cool, see you then! Bye!" She nods before bouncing across the room.

"You're not going to go though, right? Aidan said you were straight except for the final? I'm sure he'll ace you for the quiz," Peyton presses.

My eyes well up with tears. "He's not doing well."

"I heard…Sky…" Peyton's concerned blue eyes bore into mine.

"He misses me too."

"I could have told you that."

"Maybe I should go."

"To class?"

I nod. "I want to see him. I miss him…"

"Skyler…what's that going to solve? It's going to make it hurt worse. You can't look at his Instagram but you can see him in person?"

"Hey guys."

I'm thankful for the interruption even if it is Dave wielding three shots.

"Thanks," I say as I down the shot without waiting. The

clear liquid burns the entire way down, but frankly, it's easier to swallow than Lily's words or the idea of seeing Aidan again.

My hair and eyelashes are perfectly curled, my lips bright red, and my eyelids expertly lined. I'd chosen a dress under my leather jacket that showcased my legs with heels to give me some height. I'm not sure what the purpose of my get-up is. Do I want Aidan's attention? Do I want to distract him? Do I want to appear like I've moved on? That I'm not hurting? I'm not sure, but when he walks into the room, time stands still. His eyes lock on mine instantly, as if he's been looking at my chair every class to see if I showed up. A ghost of a smile finds his lips before he turns to address the class.

His hair is a little longer and he has more facial hair than I remember. *Fuck, he looks good. Really good.* I squeeze my legs together as I try to ignore the ache between them. But then I remember the ache in my chest and decide focusing on the thump in my sex is better than the one in my heart.

Per Lily's tip, we do have a pop quiz and while I know all the answers I can't help myself from writing something else after the essay on the third page. I know Aidan grades all his students' papers himself, opting to not have a teacher's assistant, so I don't have to worry about anyone else seeing it.

I miss you. I hope you're well.

For a second I regret it. Is this a bad idea? What if he doesn't ever see it? Or what if he does, but doesn't care? I've written it in pen so there's no going back. I rest my head in my right hand as I hear the shuffle of people getting up. I know I shouldn't wait until the end, to be the last person to turn in their test, but as people file out of class one by one, I long for a second alone with him. I'd caught his gaze more than a few times, and I felt it on me even more times. *Look away, Aidan, please.*

The minute hand ticks to the ten, indicating the end of class, and I watch as the last few people in class scribble their last few answers in a panic.

"Time's up, everyone left please bring your papers up." I'm frozen in place. I'd been done since the first twenty minutes and I can't force myself to get up. I'm terrified of seeing Aidan. I don't know how long I stare at my quiz, wishing that I could just disappear when I feel his presence next to me. I look up, avoiding his gaze and notice that we're alone. "Skyler," he whispers.

"I...a little birdie told me we were having a pop quiz. I wasn't sure...I mean...I thought I should be here." My voice is timid and barely above a whisper.

"I would have told you if you needed to. I was going to give you an A." His tone matches mine. I slide my quiz across the desk slowly.

"Well, now you can give me a real grade."

"You look nice," he tells me, ignoring my comments.

"Thank you."

"Did you wear this...for me?"

I rub my forehead nervously. "Yes...I don't know...maybe?"

"Skyler, look at me." I do as he tells me and I feel my heart actually melt in my chest. He is so beautiful, it almost hurts to look at him. Thank God he's hurting because I don't think I would be able to handle seeing him smile with those beautiful dimples. He swallows and collects my quiz in his hand. "Have a good Thanksgiving." He stands up without another word. I watch as he puts the papers in his bag and disappears from the room leaving me all alone. I doubt he even made it out of the building before the tears are flying down my face.

The drive to Connecticut is long as fuck. Six hours of highway upon highway. I would be sitting in silence if it weren't for the fact that I would probably run my car off the road, fully hypnotized by the highway. But every song makes me think of Aidan, somehow. The love songs make me think of him. The happy songs make me think of us. The songs that speak of heartbreak and pain make me think of him. By the time I pull into my driveway later that night, I've cried four separate times and am currently in a fit of sobs. I don't know how long I've sat in my car with my head in my hands when I smell lavender filling my nostrils. "Oh Bella, come in." My mother's nickname for me only makes me cry harder.

The next thing I know, it's morning and I'm in my bed at home. I've been looking forward to this trip, hoping that some time away from D.C. would do me some good. The Skyler that lived in Connecticut didn't know Aidan. She didn't love him with every fiber of her being. I sit up in bed and rub my face before immediately checking my phone like I do every morning. Hoping, praying for a message from Aidan. At this point, I would take a drunk text he more than likely regretted the next morning. I just want some connection to him.

Maybe it's time to reactivate my Instagram.

My door opens and my sister comes through it. My twenty-one year old sister is a senior at UConn and lives at home because she just didn't quite crave the adventure I did. She stays in our guest house because she told herself—and everyone else—that she didn't want to force any extra expenses on our parents. But I know the truth: she was scared and needs my mother for *everything*.

"You look like shit." She pushes her glasses further up on her nose and tucks a long, dark brown lock behind her ear.

"Thanks. You can exit the way you entered." I point at the door and lay back down, wishing that sleep could claim me before Serena Mitchell can throw in more of her two cents about my appearance.

She hops on my bed and smacks my body covered by my plush comforter. "Tell me about D.C. Do you love it?"

"What part of get out are you not getting, Rena? In case you haven't noticed, I'm not in the mood for our bitchy banter." My sister and I have an interesting relationship. It's just her and me, and I'll admit I spent a lot of my life being the spoiled little sister. She had been two when I was born, and I probably spent the next fifteen years demanding mom and dad's attention. I understand her resentment. I own it. But it doesn't stop me from giving it as good as I got it.

She pouts. "I'm going to go to the mall today. Do you want to come? You look like you could use some fresh air. Seriously, did you stop showering in D.C.?"

"I don't want to go to the mall."

"Why?" she whines.

"Because Serena, I don't. Go away!"

"Because some boy broke your heart again? I swear Skyler…"

"At least boys fucking like me, now go away!"

I know it was a low blow, and something that Serena is sensitive about, but I just *can't*. I'm pretty sure Serena is a virgin, but it isn't something she talks about. She's beautiful and an exact replica of my mother, yet she feels like she repels the opposite sex. *Well, she is kind of rude to anyone that shows her any interest, so I guess that doesn't help.* "God, you're a bitch."

"I learned from the best. Please remove yourself from my room."

I don't feel her moving so I kick her to drag my point home. "Ow! Listen. What's that shit you're always preaching, huh? *La vita va avanti*, Skyler. You've gotten through heartbreak before, you can again."

My heart thumps in my chest. "This is different," I whisper and feel bad for being mean to Serena when maybe she is just trying to help the only way she knows how.

"How?"

"He's the one," I murmur. I expect a snort or a snarky comment or for her to remind me that at one point I thought Gabriel was the one. Instead, I hear a gasp.

"How do you know?"

"It's hard to explain, Serena. It's just a feeling."

"Well, what happened?"

"You'll judge me." And she would. Serena took goody two shoes to a completely different level. She played by the rules, always.

"No…I won't."

"Liar."

"When do I lie about anything? It's what gets me into trouble."

This is true, Serena has no problem telling you the truth about everything and she rarely hides her opinions.

"He's my teacher."

"What! Sky…"

I sit up and stare at her. "I fell in love with my teacher."

Her hazel eyes are full of worry and confusion. "Holy shit. Is he…like old?"

"Older than me." I shrug.

"Obviously. But I mean…like…dad's age? *Older* than dad?" I'll admit I'm surprised that this is her first question.

"No no." I snort. "He's thirty-two."

"Oh." She lets out a sigh and her eyes dart around the room as if she's nervous. "So, what happened?"

"CGU prohibits any kind of relationship between students and teachers."

"Well, yeah, just while you have him though, right?"

See! What kind of shit is CGU on? Are they the only school with this bullshit rule? "Nope. All four years."

"Well, that seems excessive."

"Who you tellin?"

"I'm sorry, Skyler." She puts her hand over mine and gives me a sad smile. "And I'm sorry for being such a dick to you over that guy in Italy. I couldn't understand…I didn't understand. But I do now. I'm sorry that I was so mean to you."

I snort. "Yeah, but I'm used to it."

Her face falls into a frown. "I hate how we are sometimes."

"Me too." I wonder where this is coming from though. "Wait…" I snap my head towards her. "If you're saying you couldn't understand before but you can now, does that mean…"

"I met someone." She grins from ear to ear and for the first time, there's a happy thump in my chest.

"Oh my God, Serena!"

"He's amazing. I've never felt this way ever."

"Tell me about him! Wait…does this mean you're not a virgin anymore?" I shake my shoulders at her and giggle.

She blushes and turns away and I have to say this might be the first time I've ever seen my sister embarrassed. "How did you know…?"

I cock my head to the side and raise an eyebrow. "I know things. Also, mom had my ass on birth control, but not you."

She bites her bottom lip and nods. "Oh my God, how have I gone this long without knowing what an orgasm feels like?"

"You didn't masturbate?" I raise my eyebrows at her. "God, where the hell did you come from?" I throw my covers off the bed and trudge towards my ensuite bathroom with her in tow.

"I didn't know what I was doing, I tried but…I wasn't doing it right."

"Who masturbates wrong? Just do what feels good."

"Nothing felt right." She crosses her arms and I pull out the necessary items to wash my face.

"Well, I'm glad that you've finally come. That must be why you're not so uptight."

"Totally. I felt like the weight of the world was just lifted from my shoulders and all my troubles just melted away."

"Sounds about right. What do mom and dad think?"

"Mom and Dad don't exactly…know."

I'm shocked that my sister hadn't run to our mother while she was still coming down from the orgasmic high. "Oh? Why the secrets?"

"Ummm…well…remember how you asked me not to judge you?"

"Oh God, who is it?"

"Sky…" she warns.

"Okay, no judgment." My heart races thinking about the fact that if Serena is asking me not to judge then it means she's broken a rule.

"It's Landon."

"Landon..." I trail off as I run through a list of guys I know in my mind. "Is that supposed to mean something to me?"

"West..." She trails off again.

"Still lost."

"God, Sky. Are you that self-involved? What is Dad's firm called?"

"Mitchell, Frank, and..." I trail off before my eyes go wide. "OH MY FUCKING GOD! You're fucking Dad's partner!"

"SHUT THE FUCK UP!" She puts a hand over my mouth and squeezes.

I squeal under her hand and when she lets go I squeal louder. "Oh my God!" I giggle. "Dad is going to freak."

"Dad isn't going to do anything, because he's not going to find out." She shoots me a pointed look. *Like I would ever rat her out.*

"Well, if you love him, you're going to have to. And hold up...isn't he married?"

"He's... going through a divorce." I watch as she twists a gold ring on her finger that I don't recognize. *Is that like a promise ring? Perhaps now is not the time to delve into how far along on this divorce process, Mr. Wilson really is.*

"Oh God, Serena...you're in worse shape than me."

"Gee, thanks." She groans and slaps my arm.

"How long?"

"I'm interning at dad's office for the semester and... well..."

"An office tryst, how *hot*."

"It's not. It's scary as fuck. I swear to God, Dad has almost caught us twice."

"Does he sneak into the guest house and make you

scream?" I giggle, so happy that one, my sister is getting some *and* two, that she finally got that stick out of her ass.

"Skyler," she huffs. "Don't be so crude."

"Oh, there's my sister. I was beginning to wonder who the hell you were."

The rest of the morning is spent hearing more than I think I ever wanted to know about a man that is only a few years younger than our father. It is the longest I've gone without thinking about Aidan, but my bliss is interrupted by an email.

You have a way with words, Miss Mitchell – A

I see that Aidan uploaded my grade for the quiz and it's the only comment that makes me believe he's seen my note.

Does that mean he misses me too?

Aidan

*F*UCK, I MISS SKYLER.

The thought hits me like a ton of bricks every time I think about her. I've been actively trying to avoid her and it's been working out well. I don't go to the quad, *ever*, and she deleted her Instagram so I'm not staring at it for several hours a day like I was in the beginning. I've only driven by her place once…well, twice. But I hadn't seen her. I was holding somewhat strong, and then she walked into my class and I almost risked everything. The words were sitting on the tip of my tongue.

Everyone out, except you, I was going to say as I pointed at Skyler.

I had an inkling she had written something on her quiz and I had a moment of happiness that she also missed me. But it was quickly replaced by the fact that nothing mattered. It doesn't matter that I miss Skyler or that she misses me. I can't have her.

And then as I read her words for what feels like the hundredth time in an hour, it hits me. It *does* matter. Skyler's feelings matter a great deal to me. I love her and I'm not letting her get away.

But there is something I need to do before I could go after her.

It's the evening before Thanksgiving break when my computer beeps with the sound of an incoming email.

Dr. Reed,

We are thrilled that you've decided to join the team. Pending a background check, we look forward to seeing you in the spring.

Dr. Richard Matthews
Dean of Brookdale University School of Law

My heart lurches forward, grateful that my mentor pulled in the favors of his life to get me an accelerated phone interview at one of the top law schools in D.C. My fingers itch to call Skyler to tell her the good news. That this is the end. That we can be together the second the semester is over, but I need to see her face. I need to tell her in person so we can consummate properly. So she would know that I have no plans of ever letting her go again. That I'm *all in*.

I hit send on my resignation that I've drafted up days ago to both Human Resources and Dr. Hendricks before printing out a copy that I will be sliding into their mailboxes tomorrow, complete with my signature.

After winter break, I'm out.

I'm in my office packing up to head home for Thanksgiving break when there's a knock on my door. "Door's open." I know it can't possibly be a student, as I told them that one on one office hours were over. Not to mention, I don't know a student alive that isn't high-tailing it home for break this Friday afternoon. We are one of the few schools that don't have class at all during Thanksgiving week, giving students a nine-day break.

"Dr. Reed," I hear from the door and I look up to see Dr. Hendricks standing in the frame, his eyeglasses atop his head and his arms crossed against his sweater vest, "heading home?"

"Yep." Thanksgiving is huge in the Reed family. Relatives come from all over; my parents host every year. Christmas is more low-key, especially since neither my sister or I have kids, but Thanksgiving is a huge ordeal.

"I got your email."

I nod. "I left a hard copy in your inbox."

"You weren't happy here, son?" He slides his hands into his pockets, and if I didn't know any better I would say he feels bad about it.

I shoot him a look and shake my head. "It wasn't that, necessarily."

"Aidan," he takes a step into my office and closes the door behind him, "off the record."

"Off the record?" I contemplate telling him the truth, but I remember I still have another month. "I just don't think this is the right fit for me."

"Does this have to do with a student?"

"No," I answer immediately. Skyler is so much more than just my student. *Hell, I wouldn't call her my student at all.* She taught me more than I ever taught her. "The students are great."

He looks at me for a minute like he's trying to read me, and I hope I don't give anything away. "Well, I wish you the best, Doctor Reed, and please let me know if you need a recommendation in the future. You are a great teacher."

"I appreciate that." *Not that I need it.*

"Enjoy your break."

"Same to you, Doctor Hendricks."

The drive to Connecticut is slightly shorter than the one to Massachusetts, but not by much. By the time I make it to Connecticut, it's late and I'm exhausted. My plans to see Skyler tonight changed due to sitting in traffic two separate times on the drive. Now, it's close to ten and I don't think that showing up at their house this late is the way to get on Preston Mitchell's good side.

Hi sir, I'm in love with your daughter and I want to marry her. Oh also, I'm her teacher for the next month.

I begin to regret the trek I made here. My only thoughts were getting to Skyler, so the thought had escaped me that perhaps her parents wouldn't be too thrilled. That they won't be on board with the age difference. I pull into a shopping center for some gas and a Red Bull when something behind it catches my eye. I don't know where I've seen it before but I know that I recognize it.

Greenwich Artistry.

I pull out my phone and am grateful I'd had the oversight to screenshot a few pictures from Skyler's Instagram before she deleted it. I find the picture of her tattoo and notice the Geotag.

That's where she got her tattoo.

I pull out of the station and into the parking lot, and I'm surprised that it's still open. I open the door and am stunned at how quiet it is. I'd been to a few tattoo parlors in my day, when Chace got his and even once with my sister, Beth, who had at least ten at this point.

I don't have anything against them. I just never had something that I cared enough about to get permanently etched on my body. Nothing that was so much ingrained in my DNA that I felt the need to have it ingrained in my skin as well.

Until Skyler.

"Honey, we are about to close up for the night," an older woman who looks like she should run a bakery or a florist or a daycare enters the room. There isn't a tattoo in sight and her hair is pulled back into a low bun. She has pearl studs in both ears as well as a string of them around her neck.

I guess I really am in Connecticut.

"Right…do you think you have time for one more?"

"What were you thinking, handsome?" She crosses her arms and pulls her glasses out of her pants pocket before sliding them on her face. "And where?"

"Maybe a few words? On my arm?" I ask. "Or here, maybe?" I point to my side and trail my hand down my ribs. I had never considered a tattoo, and now here I am impulsively deciding to get one.

"This is a popular place for the guys. What do you want it to say?"

Ten minutes later, underneath a bandage and the promise to not get it wet for at least forty-eight hours, I'm back in my car.

I look at the photo that I'd asked her to take for me and I smile.

Amor Vincit Omnia.

Love Conquers All.

I love Skyler. I'd broken all the rules to be with her, and then I'd broken us both by ending it. But in the end, our love could overcome any obstacle.

I pull into a quaint hotel, remembering once again that I'm in Connecticut. I barely make it through the "orientation," my eyes fighting to close with the tour of each room of the bed and breakfast. I just hope to God that her parents are welcoming and allow me to stay with them, because I am not about to stay in this *Alice in Wonderland* themed acid trip longer than one night.

Unless of course, Skyler stays here with me. My cock springs to life thinking about our reunion. I hadn't been inside of her in almost four weeks and my body has noticed. I have a month's worth of tension that I need to release inside of her. I look down at my phone to see if Skyler has emailed me back after the email I sent letting her know that she'd gotten an A on the quiz. I hope she understands that I saw her message as well. Our emails are monitored, so I can't very well say that I miss her too. I just hope that she read between the lines.

I don't even bother to take off my clothes after kicking off my shoes before my eyes flutter closed and sleep takes me.

Tomorrow, I get my girl back.

I pull into the driveway of the large Colonial mansion where Skyler lives. I assumed that she was well off when everyone went on and on about her father, but I wasn't expecting *this* level of wealth. The driveway is long and paved with grey stone, lined with flowers all the way up to the house. I notice two garages off to the side that have two Audis, a Maserati and a Benz. On the other side of the house, I see a smaller house with two other cars, one of which I recognize—Skyler's BMW—and I wonder if she stays in the guest house. I step out of my car, wishing that I'd brought flowers or something. I've been anxious all morning, for a reason I'm not sure of. Do I think she'll turn me down? Tell me that she's come to her senses and she's over me? *Is she over me?*

I make my way up the steps taking them two at a time. I let out a deep breath and raise my hand to knock when the door flies open and I'm staring at Skyler's face. *Just...different.*

"Holy shit." Her hair is longer and darker and she has thick-rimmed square glasses that sit in front of hazel eyes, versus Skyler's dark brown ones.

"Well, I guess there's no question that I have the right house." I chuckle as I assume I'm looking at Serena, Skyler's older sister. "I assume you're Serena?"

"And you're the teacher." She raises her eyebrows and a smile finds her lips.

"She told you about me?"

She nods and motions me inside. "I can't believe you're here. She's going to freak."

I let out a breath. *If she told her sister, that means she must still want me, right?* I know her relationship with her sister is weird, but I also know she's still honest with her. "How is she?"

She purses her lips and leads me into the kitchen. "She misses you."

"I—" I start when another woman enters the room and I freeze, gathering that this must be Skyler's mother. Warm brown eyes meet mine and a smile pulls at the corner of her mouth as she looks me over.

"Oh. Hello. I didn't realize we had company. Rena, you can't give me any notice? I would have made a lasagna. *Sinceramente, Bella.*" *Honestly, Bella.*

"She calls you both Bella?" I ask Serena. She scoffs and puts a hand up.

"I was Bella, first. I'm the original Bella." She turns to her Mother. "I didn't know he was coming, Mama. He's here for Skyyyyyler." She hops on the marble counter and swings her legs like she's ready to watch a show.

Skyler's mother furrows her brow and looks up at me. *"Oh mio!" Oh my!* She puts a hand over her chest. *"E'vecchio." He's old.* I swallow, understanding what she said, and decide now might be the time, to let them know I understand Italian.

"È un piacere conoscerla, signora." It's nice to meet you, ma'am. I hold my hand out for hers. Her eyes widen as she extends her hand to me and I kiss it. As soon as I let it go, she wraps her arms around me.

"Oh dio mio, lui è Italiano" Oh my God, he's Italian!

"Right, so stop talking about him," Serena laughs as Mrs. Mitchell lets me go.

"I'm not Italian, I just found the language fascinating, so I took it in high school and college and studied abroad in Italy in college."

She looks at me like I've just told her the secrets of the universe. "Wow. Well, sit sit, are you hungry?"

"No...well, I..." I look from where she appeared from, wondering where the other Mitchell lady is.

"She's on a run," Serena answers, as if she can hear my thoughts. "She always runs when she's...not herself," she tells me and Mrs. Mitchell gives me a look.

"Are you why my daughter is not…herself?" She looks at me. "You hurt my Bella?"

My heart bangs in my chest. "Not…not in the way you're thinking," I tell her. Serena gives me a look that her mother misses and shakes her head. *Right, so she doesn't know the details.*

"Do you love her?" her mother asks.

"Yes."

"Do you live in D.C.? Do…do you go to CGU?" I can hear the sentiment behind her words. *I understand people go back to school later in life all the time. But something tells me that's not this story.*

Our conversation is halted by a door opening and closing and footsteps coming closer to the kitchen. We are all quiet as Skyler's sister and mom stare at me, and we all wait for Skyler to enter the room. I hear her getting closer, and then she's walking through the entryway, but her eyes are fixed on her phone with her headphones in her ear. The kitchen is large and wide and somehow she hasn't noticed that we're all staring at her. She looks up and sees her mom first and she pulls her headphones out. "What? Sorry, did you say something?"

"Come on, Mama. Let's give them some privacy." Her eyes dart to me and Skyler follows her gaze, dropping her phone with a yelp.

"Holy fu—" Her eyes are wide and her mouth ajar in shock.

"Language, Bella," her mother says as Serena ushers her out.

"Ai—Aidan? What are you doing here? In Connecticut…in my kitchen?" She looks around and now that her eyes are on me and we are alone in the room, I can take the time to note her delicious workout gear. Tight leggings squeeze her legs and a tiny lime green sports bra covers her perky tits. Her hair is pulled up into a bun, but several strands have escaped and her skin is glistening with sweat. My cock wakes up, seeing her so close and breathing in her scent. She must see the look I'm giving her because she bites her lip. "Aidan, stop looking at me like that."

"Why?" I take a step towards her. "I think we've been over that you are mine. Do you need a reminder?"

"I...I didn't..." Her voice falters and I take another step towards her, wrapping my hand around her and pulling her into my arms.

"You are *mine*. Skyler. *Forever.*" I rub her cheek as the tears well in her eyes. *"Sei il grande amore della mia vita."* *You are the love of my life.* "And I don't want to live without you in it anymore."

"Aidan, but..."

"Tell me you feel the same," I ask her. "Tell me your feelings haven't changed." I pull her hand towards me and hold it to my cheek before I press a kiss to her palm.

"Why are you doing this to me?" she cries. "You know we can't. It's not fair for you to dangle *this* in front of me. And then what after Thanksgiving? We go back to the way things were?" The tears are flying down her face and I can't wait until I can kiss them away.

"We can, Skyler." I cup her face and wipe the tears from under her eyes. "I resigned from CGU."

"Wh—what?" Her eyes are as wide as saucers.

"I quit. I'm finishing out the semester and then I'm done. I won't be there in the spring."

"Wait...you quit...for me?"

"I can't think of a better reason."

"But...where will you go? Back to Boston?"

I can't leave you, baby. "No. I got another teaching job in

D.C. I called in a few favors. I'm going to teach at Brookdale Law School."

"Oh my God." She puts a hand over her mouth and stares up at me. "This is real…"

"Baby, it was never *not* real," I tell her as I wrap my arms around her.

"But…we can be together?"

"Forever, I hope," I whisper against her lips and she gasps, granting me access to her mouth. My tongue darts out in search of hers and she meets it with equal urgency, needing me as desperately as I need her.

"Aidan…" she whimpers as I lift her into my arms and sit at the table in her kitchen. She straddles me instantly, rubbing against me and mewling like a cat in heat. I release her mouth after what feels like forever and find her chest, licking her skin clean of the sweat that coats her.

"You taste so fucking sweet," I whisper against her.

"I love you so much. Promise me, we'll never be apart again," she begs. I bite her nipple through her sports bra before pulling the material down slightly and pressing my lips to the skin to soothe the sting.

"Never. These few weeks were rough. I missed you every day, princess."

"Me too." She rubs her nose against mine. "I thought about you all the time." She blinks the tears from her eyes. "Come shower with me."

"In your parent's house, while your sister and your mother are up walking around? Think again, Sky." As much as the idea of being in an enclosed space with a naked and wet Skyler appeals to me, I value my life a bit more than that. *God knows where her father is.*

She furrows her brow as she thinks of an alternative. I'm

just about to mention that we can go to my hotel when her eyes light up. "We can go to the guest house. It's where Serena lives."

"Your sister?"

"It'll be fine. Trust me."

I remember the fresh ink that still can't get wet. "Well, maybe I can just watch you shower."

"You don't want to join me? Aidan, we're going to fuck in the shower. I just want to get clean first," she says sarcastically, like I don't know that's where she was going with her plan.

"No, I know. I just…I can't shower at the moment."

"Oh…kay? Why?"

"I uhh…I got a tattoo." I find myself hoping that she likes it. That it turns her on as much as hers turns me on.

She gasps and looks me over from head to toe, like she missed it. "Where? What? When?"

"My ribcage and last night. I went to Greenwich Artistry."

Her lips form an 'o' shape and she smiles. "That's where I got mine!"

"I know." I kiss her hand and help her to her feet so I can show her.

"I didn't know you wanted a tattoo?"

"I didn't know a lot of things about myself until I met you." I lift my shirt and motion for her to lift the bandage.

"Love conquers all," she says softly as she traces the perimeter of the ink with her fingertip. "It's in Italian."

"You don't miss a thing." I chuckle and she looks up at me, clearly ignoring my sarcasm.

"Because…of me?"

"You know they say that getting your partner's name on you is bad luck…so I decided against that. But I thought…I wanted something that made me think of you. *And us.* Falling in love with you was so completely out of my control. I *never* saw you coming." I brush a strand of hair from her face. "And now I can't picture my life without you."

"Aidan..." she chokes out. "I love it. I love you!" She presses a kiss to the skin just under the tattoo before I let my shirt down.

"I love you too, Skyler," I whisper in her ear as she wraps her arms around me. We hold each other for a little longer, just soaking in the feeling of being together again for the first time in a month.

"Well, you can watch me shower if you want. I give it thirty seconds before you crack." She winks.

I don't necessarily have to creep down the hallway, as her bedroom is on the opposite side of the house as her parents' bedroom, but it doesn't stop me from being as quiet as I can. Her father, who is out of town, is flying back early in the morning upon hearing about Skyler's new boyfriend who was caught *"feeling up my baby in the kitchen!"* Skyler assured me that she had her father wrapped around her finger and not to worry, but... I'm worried.

I'm scared shitless.

The plan for the shower show that I was supposed to get never happened after Serena and her mother intercepted us as we tried to leave. Then, we tried to sneak away to have a quickie in my Jeep, or go to my hotel but Skyler's mother proved to be quite the cockblock. It was one of those times that I forgot that Skyler was only nineteen, and maybe her mother wasn't quite ready to be privy to her daughter having sex.

That is how I got here, creeping down the hallway to Skyler's room so I can finally reunite with my girlfriend properly. I slide into Skyler's room to find her sitting up with the largest smile on her face. She's off the bed before the door is even fully shut with her legs completely wrapped around me. "Oh my God, finally!" she whispers in my ear and kisses the space there, dragging her teeth over my neck. I don't get a good look at her, only enough to know that she's completely naked and I grip her butt as I carry her to her bed.

"Fuck. I can't wait to get inside of you, baby," I growl in her ear. "Can you be quiet, princess? I promise when we get back to D.C. you can be as loud as you want, but tonight you have to be quiet, okay?"

"Yes. Yes, I promise I'll be quiet, just touch me." She moves out of my arms and lies in the center of her bed, her legs completely spread, and opens her sex for me. I scan her body as I shed my clothes at rapid speed.

"Fuck. I missed you," I tell her while I move onto the bed with her. My lips start at her left ankle, and I drag them up her leg. She mewls and raises her hips towards my mouth. I do the same on her other leg, not touching the space we both need.

"Aidan, fuck. Kiss me."

"Ask me nicely."

"*Please*," she grits out. "Please. I've missed you so much."

"You have no idea. I've been dreaming about this perfect pussy for weeks. Salivating for the taste of you. Fuck. I am going to suck you dry, Skyler."

"Oh God!" She puts a pillow over her face to muffle her moans just as I make the final descent over her sweet center. I don't hesitate another second before my mouth is at the apex of her thighs, my tongue swirling around her precious cunt while her legs quake under the force. The hair on her pussy tickles my lips and I welcome the feeling that I haven't had in weeks. I thought I wanted to take my time, tease and torture her until she begs for release, but the second her flavors hit my tongue, I know I *need* her orgasm. I need to drink from her. I need her to drench my face.

My hands reach under her bottom and I grip her cheeks hard as I ravage her pussy like it's my last meal. I know first-hand that she loves when I eat her this way. Not soft languid strokes, but rough rapid ones where I don't think about coming up for air. The times I completely immerse myself in her. Her essence, her juices, *her*. I eat her with an intensity that has her shuddering almost instantly, and then I keep going. Kissing and licking her through the violent orgasm that rips her apart. Her clit pulses under my tongue but I don't stop, knowing I won't be sated until I feel it at least two more times.

And then I'll fuck her with my cock.

I press my fingers inside of her, hooking around that spot that I'd only been able to find on her. It's like I'm programmed to know exactly what she likes. To know how to make her body hum and sizzle and come alive. It's like only I have the manual to Skyler's body and I've spent years memorizing it.

"Aidan," she whines, and I know she's building after the orgasm she'd just whimpered through. She knows what's in store for her. "More…more…" She pulls at my hair, but simultaneously pushes me deeper inside of her. I nip at her clit with my teeth, sucking it into my mouth, and I'm greeted with an explosion of flavors flooding my mouth.

"Oh my God." She clamps down around my head and shudders over and over as she climaxes.

Fuck. I love when she squirts. I groan, savoring her taste in my mouth and drinking her from the fountain that flows from this violent orgasm. I suck down everything her body offers before I pull back and stare at the redness forming across her pussy. I kiss her pubic bone, the top of her mound and the space on her thighs closest to her pussy. I lift her pelvis and kiss the space just below her anus and trail kisses back up until I'm back at her clit. "Again, baby?"

"No…your dick. I need you inside of me." She removes the pillow, and her eyes are trained on me as she tweaks her nipples. *Fuck, I want to suck on them.*

I oblige her request and slide inside her pussy. I'm instantly hit with the feeling that I'm ready to come. "Fuck, Sky. It's too much. You're too tight and it's been too long and…" The feeling snakes down my spine making me shiver and every hair stands up on end. I can't even thrust again knowing that I'll come the second I feel the friction of her walls rubbing against my cock.

"Baby, I've already come twice. It's your turn." My arms begin to shake with the force of the impending orgasm and I prepare myself to let go.

"I shouldn't come inside you," I tell her as I begin to thrust again.

"Yes, you should," she murmurs and she squeezes down on me to confirm her thoughts.

"Skyler…" I groan as I push in and out of her. I squeeze my eyes shut, feeling my dick harden more with every stroke. She shudders underneath me and I can tell her orgasm is building within. I feel her toes pointing and flexing every few thrusts and I know that means she's nearing the edge. I pull her to sit up in my lap so she can bounce on my cock and also so my lips can suck on her nipples. "Come for me, baby."

She wraps her arms around my neck and presses my face to her chest. "Fuck…I'm right…*there.*" She sinks her nails into my shoulders. "Oh fuck. Oh fuck. Oh FUCK," she says a little too loud, but I can't be bothered to care when she's soaking my dick with her cunt. "I love you so much," she repeats over and over as she comes down from her high. And within seconds, her words coupled with her orgasm triggers my own and I begin pumping into her, rope after rope of thick cum deep into her womb. The thoughts of pulling out have been completely forgotten.

Fuck.

I'll be shocked if she's not pregnant by the end of first semester.

Epilogue

Aidan

Four Years Later

"Oh God, right there, *Doctor Reed*," Skyler calls out just a little too loudly and I peek over my shoulder to make sure that no one happens to be around.

"Shhh, princess, there are people right outside," I murmur against her ear as I glide my fingers over her slippery clit.

"You shhh. Make me come," she sasses and I resist the chuckle sitting in my throat. Her eyes are squeezed together, her teeth dig into her bottom lip as she thrusts her hips onto my fingers while she holds her gown up around her waist. Her cap had long fallen to the floor the second I slammed her against the wall of the stairwell in the law building, a place where we'd had sex more than a few times over the years. Even after I'd quit working for Camden Graf, we would sneak in here and relive our forbidden trysts when the mood struck, or when Skyler was drunk.

"I fucked you twice this morning, and ate your pussy in the shower; how are you still this horny?" I chuckle in her ear as she rides my fingers and chases the orgasm that is only a few seconds away. *I know why, I'm just trying to probe it out of her.*

Skyler Mitchell, my former student and also the love of my life, is pregnant. *And evidently my cock is her biggest consistent craving.*

We are having a baby.

Skyler was ready to get pregnant the second we got back together, and while I was in a place in my life that I was also ready, I wanted her to get through school first. So, after basically forcing her down and making her get an IUD since she proved to be the absolute *worst* at remembering to take her pills, she agreed to wait until after graduation. Somehow, that turned into having it removed early during winter break because *"even if I get pregnant now, I still won't give birth until after graduation."*

My dick, who only heard that I was able to come inside Skyler with no protection whatsoever was in total agreement.

"Are you complaining?" She raises an eyebrow at me cheekily. "I thought you liked making me come."

"I live to make you come, Skyler. I just know you. And you're keeping something from me." I stop fingering her, knowing that this conversation isn't one we can have while I'm knuckle deep inside of her. "And we have to get out there. Commencement starts in ten minutes." My fingers find my lips and I suck her essence from them greedily. My eyes peek out of the window that is over Skyler's head. Parents, students, and faculty have begun taking their seats for the ceremony.

"You're keeping something from me too," she answers, without a care in the world that her college graduation starts in ten minutes and she is nowhere near her assigned seat. The College of Justice ceremony is just outside of the law building on the lawn, so we wouldn't have to go far, but I am *sure* her parents are looking for her, the way that Serena has been blowing up her phone since we snuck away. *Fuck, Skyler's parents will murder me if we're late.*

My mind goes back to her comment about keeping something from her. *I know she knows.* I tried my hardest to keep a secret, but Skyler is just so Goddamn nosy and she can read me like a book. It's hard to live with someone and keep a secret from them when they can read it all over your face. I actually think one of the times I was going to look at rings, I told her I was going to have lunch with my mother—*my mother, who lives in Boston.*

I narrow my eyes at her. "So, we both have secrets then…"

"Is it a secret when I know what it is?" She puts her hands on her hips

"Is it if I know too?" I quip.

She gasps but immediately shuts her mouth. "You don't know anything." She narrows her eyes at me.

"Oh? Let's just say for argument's sake, that I don't notice that you haven't had your period this month…or last month," I shrug. "But, my little lush, I haven't seen you consume one drop of alcohol in weeks. And while I know you've been studying your ass off, I do know that you wouldn't pass on the multiple tequila shots I did last night with your sister and your father."

She huffs and stomps her foot. "You're a dick!"

I chuckle, but I know it's time to nip this in the bud. Skyler can find a way to surprise me for our next baby. "Is that any way to talk to the father of your child?"

"You know I love tequila. *You* don't even like tequila! You were just trying to torture me because you know I can't have it!" She pouts but I don't miss the smile that plays on her lips.

"Baby…" I cock my head to the side and the tears fill her eyes instantly.

"How long have you known?"

"A couple weeks."

"Why didn't you say anything?"

"I thought you'd come to me!" I push her against the wall and raise her gown as well as her dress underneath to press my hands to her soft, bare skin. "Say it."

She smiles through her tears and all thoughts that maybe she isn't as excited about having a baby as I am, go out the window. "We're having a baby."

I swallow past the lump in my throat as I stare down at this woman who's changed me in so many ways. I lift her off the ground and hold her tight against me. I press my forehead to hers and let out a breath.

My hand finds her arm and I rub her tattoo, a gesture we've both started doing when things are intense and we can't find the words.

La vita va avanti.

Life goes on.

And now we've created new life.

"Skyler." I'm not sure if it's the news that Skyler and I are going to be parents. Or maybe it's because it's her graduation day and I'm planning to ask her tonight anyway. Or maybe it's because we're back in the building where our romance began, but the words fall from my lips before I can stop them.

"Mi vuoi sposare?"

Will you marry me?

The End.

Author's Note

Thank you so much for reading! I hope you enjoyed Skyler and Aidan as much as I loved writing them. A number of you know that I got my start writing about shenanigans in college. Years later and I still look back at those four years with fond (blurry) memories. I knew I'd always wanted to write a teacher/student romance because I do love a forbidden love story. In my writing, I realized I had more college stories to tell and so with some help from my beta team, *campus tales* was born. I have a few other stories floating around my brain and I can't wait to share them with you.

All hot.
All potentially forbidden.
All college.
Let's do this.

Acknowledgements

To my beta baes: Carmel, Helen, Kristene & Leslie, you guys are unbelievable! Thank you for your constant support. For keeping me on track and reigning me in when I need it. For seeing the vision, and helping me achieve it. Your support is invaluable to me. So much love.

Jeanette: You ROCKED this cover. I love it so much, and I can't wait to see more of your magic!

Kristen and Stacey: We're now three for three! I don't know what I would do without you. Thank you for keeping me sane and accepting my perpetual procrastination. I think I did better this time? Thank you for always making my books beautiful in every way!

To the ladies of the *original* hive: This story is for you. I love you, always. And who knows, perhaps Sean will get a story down the line?

About the Author

Write. Wine. Work. Repeat. A look inside the mind of a not so ex-party girl's escape from her crazy life. Hailing from the Nation's Capital, Q.B. Tyler, spends her days constructing her "happily ever afters" with a twist. Romantic comedies served with a side of smut and most importantly the love story that develops despite inconvenient circumstances.

Sign up for her newsletter (http://eepurl.com/doT8EL) to stay in touch!
Qbtyler03@gmail.com

Facebook: .facebook.com/author.qbtyler

Reader Group: www.facebook.com/groups/784082448468154

Goodreads: www.goodreads.com/author/show/17506935.Q_B_Tyler

Instagram: www.instagram.com/author.qbtyler

Wordpress: qbtyler.wordpress.com

Other Works

My Best Friend's Sister

Bittersweet Surrender

Bittersweet Addiction

Spring Semester

Second Semester

Unconditional

Forget Me Not